Love is
a time of enchantment:
in it all days are fair and all fields
green. Youth is blest by it,
old age made benign:
the eyes of love see
roses blooming in December,
and sunshine through rain. Verily
is the time of true-love
a time of enchantment — and
Oh! how eager is woman
to be bewitched!

NO ESCAPE FROM LOVE

Nurse Linda Harlan fled from Boston's Riverview Hospital when Dr. Greg Arnold, the man she secretly loved, announced his engagement to another woman. She gave up nursing and the life she knew in the States and went to stay with her father in Liberia. She even let herself enjoy the attentions of wealthy playboy, Chris Osborne, and young medical researcher, Dr. Paul Raymond — but Linda found there was no escape from her solemn pledge as a nurse, and no escape from love.

BENNIE C. HALL

NO ESCAPE FROM LOVE

Complete and Unabridged

ULVERSCROFT
Leicester

First published in the
United States of America

First Large Print Edition
published July 1995

British Library CIP Data

Hall, Bennie C.
  No escape from love.—Large print ed.—
Ulverscroft large print series: romance
I. Title
813.54 [F]

ISBN 0–7089–3329–7

Published by
F. A. Thorpe (Publishing) Ltd.
Anstey, Leicestershire
Set by Words & Graphics Ltd.
Anstey, Leicestershire
Printed and bound in Great Britain by
T. J. Press (Padstow) Ltd., Padstow, Cornwall

This book is printed on acid-free paper

For Jeffrey David Hall
in fulfillment of a promise

1

LINDA woke with a start, all but smothered by a panicky feeling that the world around her was in flames. She was conscious of a whirring sound, as though giant birds were flying over to escape the holocaust, while she herself was floundering in a billowing sea that smelled precisely like strong coffee!

Cautiously she opened her eyes, and was staring straight into the most spectacular sunrise she had ever seen in her twenty-one years. Shielding her eyes against the glare, she looked at her wrist watch — an early morning habit she'd acquired upon entering nurse's training some four years ago, and was further disconcerted to find that the hands pointed to one o'clock.

Something very definitely is wrong, she told herself shakily. Only a minute ago, it was pitch dark. I couldn't possibly have slept more than a few seconds. And surely nowhere in the world does the sun have the effrontery to rise at one o'clock in the morning — or is it afternoon?

Then, with dawning consciousness, she remembered, and the pieces of what appeared to be a fantastic jigsaw puzzle began gradually to fall into place. This was *not* Judgment-Day-in-the-morning, as she'd feared; the world was not actually on fire, and, although the aroma of coffee persisted, she was not drowning. This seemingly incredible performance was simply another phenomenon peculiar to the jet age in which she was living.

The whirring noise she had mistaken for birds flying was the sound of the plane in which she was riding, as it winged its way out of the Atlantic darkness into a brilliant African sunrise. Within the space of what seemed like a few cat naps, she had moved out of the old familiar world which she had known and loved into a never-never orbit where *anything* could happen, probably *would* happen! She, Linda Harlan, registered nurse — not a flock of terrified birds — was flying away, seeking escape from an emotional holocaust that had threatened to engulf her.

Struggling for poise, she sat up as straight as her protesting joints would allow and tried to look nonchalant. A pretty colored girl, wearing the uniform of a stewardess, was bending over her with a tray containing a glass of fruit juice and a cup of steaming coffee.

"Good morning, Miss Harlan," the girl said in a softly precise voice that held the slightest trace of an accent. "Have a good rest?"

"No — uh — yes, thank you," Linda stammered, and wondered vaguely what was wrong with her tongue. "Only," she continued, forcing a smile, "I feel — well, I don't seem to be functioning properly . . ."

The stewardess nodded, smiling. "The *circadian rhythm* — but of course. Think nothing of it, Miss Harlan. It's perfectly normal to feel abnormal after a flight through several time zones and into another hemisphere. It takes a while for our built-in time clocks to adjust."

Linda managed a half-hearted grin and tried to be facetious. "Yes, I know. But for a minute I thought may-be I was losing my mind. Anyhow, it can't possibly be tomorrow morning already."

Something suspiciously like a snicker came from across the aisle. Linda knew, without looking, that the offender was the blond young man with the brash manner and outrageously long hair. He had sauntered aboard at Kennedy Airport, New York, just as the plane was about to take off, acting as though he owned and disapproved of everything in sight. Later, he had tried to start a conversation, tormenting her with such tired old clichés as:

"Where have you been all my life? And where did you get those dancing brown eyes and gorgeous red hair? Man! You must have been a beautiful baby, on account of — "

"Don't say it," Linda had groaned, pressing her hands to her ears. "It's the grandfather of all sophomoric lines."

Oh, he had been all set to make a nuisance of himself, though Linda had tried, without being insulting, to make it clear that she wanted no part of such nonsense. She had counted on being alone with her thoughts; a chance to

4

rationalize, if possible, this drastic move she was making.

For reasons she had chosen not to discuss with co-workers and friends, she had walked out on her job at Boston's Riverview Hospital, given up her career as a nurse. She had burned her bridges, severed all ties. The immediate problem was how to justify herself in her own eyes before moving on into the new life that lay ahead.

Nevertheless, the impertinent stranger had gone right on talking, giving his helpless listener a blow-by-blow account of his recent activities, his plans for the future. Irked by his chatter, Linda had scarcely touched the delectable Cornish-hen dinner that was served shortly after the jet became airborne.

His name was Christopher Osborne the Second, he'd announced gratuitously. He had come from Texas, via Dartmouth, where he had flunked his midterms. In fact, he admitted without shame, he had been thrown out of most of the best colleges in the United States of America.

"Quite a record, huh? I am what is

5

generally known as a perennial dropout; probably the oldest in captivity," he had added with a kind of devil-may-care defiance, obviously calculated to shock. "I am twenty-three years old and never been trapped."

Presently at loose ends and not wanting to fight in a war that was not of his making, he had 'mislaid' his draft card and was now en route to join his father, who was sojourning in Liberia. The 'old man,' he explained, was a retired industrialist who collected African artifacts, went on safaris, endowed hospitals and otherwise 'lived up' the fruits of a considerable fortune.

"Now let's talk about you," he'd said unexpectedly, and had proceeded to bombard Linda with questions. Where had she come from? Where was she going — and why?

Reluctantly and as briefly as possible, Linda had answered his questions. Her name was Linda Harlan, she told him, and she, too, was en route to Liberia. A native Cape Codder, she had come via Boston, where she had worked as a nurse at Riverview Hospital.

"Oh. A career girl, huh?" he had commented, regarding Linda with a mixture of amusement and disbelief. "Then how come you're traipsing off to Africa? Running away?"

"Certainly I'm not running away." Taken off guard, Linda had all but choked over the lie. It had given her some satisfaction to add, quite truthfully:

"I am going to visit my father, just as you are. Only *my* father, a mining engineer, *works* for a living."

Under no circumstances would she tell this character that she, too, was a dropout: a runaway nurse whose culpability, she supposed, was even greater than his. Unlike Christopher Osborne, she was not proud of the dubious distinction.

He had not taken offense at her pointed remark. Instead, he'd laughed, murmured something to the effect that the Osborne tribe was allergic to work, and said:

"From here on, I aim to live it up, like my old man. I may even go on a big-game hunt, just for the heck of it. Want to come along for the ride? By the way, my friends call me Chris."

"Thank you, Mr. Osborne. But I could never be interested in hunting, either big game or small. Besides, I expect to be quite busy in Monrovia," Linda had retorted in the great-lady voice which she'd found highly successful in squelching obstreperous patients and fresh orderlies.

Christopher Osborne the Second was not squelched. "Busy doing what?" he'd demanded, favoring Linda with an infuriating grin. "Cobra-catching? I understand there's a dollar a head bounty for each mamba caught in the American Embassy Compound. I've been told you can earn as much as thirty bucks a month, if you're any good at climbing. They're tree snakes, you know."

"Sorry. I wouldn't be interested," Linda had answered with all the dignity she could muster at the moment.

"Oh. Then maybe you're the bird-watching type. Only there's no percentage in that. After all, you'll have to do something to pass the time. Monrovia isn't Beacon Hill — or didn't you know?" Then, before she could think of a suitably crushing retort:

"Okay. Have it your way, Miss Touch-me-not. Me, I aim to have fun. You'll be seeing me at the various wingdings in the American Colony. I'll be in all the best stag lines — girl-watching."

"Well, have fun; only count me out," Linda had snapped, her patience at the breaking point. With that, she'd turned away from him, to stare unseeingly into the black darkness outside, and must have fallen asleep . . .

She was propelled back into the present by the voice of the stewardess saying: "It's later than you think, Miss Harlan." As the girl spoke, she placed the tray on an adjustable shelf and push-buttoned Linda's bed-for-the-night into a chair designed for comfortable daytime sitting.

"We crossed the Atlanic while you slept," she continued. "It is now six o'clock West African time. There's a time differential of five hours between here and the States. In other words, you have gained five hours."

"Yes — yes, of course. I have gained five hours." But even as she spoke, Linda could not dismiss the painful feeling that

9

she had lost those five hours, would never in a whole lifetime retrieve them. "I must have forgotten to set my wrist watch ahead."

She had not forgotten. Stubbornly, she had chosen to ignore the change in time, as if by doing so she could carry over one small remnant of the old life into the new. It was a pretty delusion, but it wasn't working.

"I should have reminded you," the stewardess said. "In a few minutes we'll be coming into Dakar, and you'll be getting your first glimpse of Africa. So fasten your seat belt, please. Here's coffee and fruit juice for now. Breakfast between Dakar and Monrovia. They're only about an hour's flying time apart . . . "

She broke off to smile and to say, "We're changing crews at Dakar, so I shan't be seeing you again." She hesitated, then said, "May I please express the hope that you'll have a pleasant stay in our beautiful Liberia? I was born there — a member of the Bassa tribe. I hope to return some day to help my people. I'm a nurse, trained in the States, and they could use me."

It was on the tip of Linda's tongue to say, "I'm a nurse, too; maybe I could help," if only for the good of her tortured soul and as a gesture of appeasement toward a nagging conscience.

Then she thought better of it. She was no longer a nurse in good standing, had no right to claim membership in the humanitarian profession. It was a sickening thought which she preferred not to explore at the moment

With an effort, she managed to swallow the lump in her throat and to say to the departing stewardess, "I'm sorry you're leaving us. Thanks for everything. You've been wonderfully kind."

The girl smiled her appreciation and hurried away to help passengers who were getting ready to leave the plane. Already the Senegalese city of Dakar was rising up out of a sun-swept sea to meet the incoming jet.

Meanwhile, with fingers that behaved precisely like thumbs, Linda fastened her seat belt, as she'd been told. Resolutely she adjusted her wrist watch in accordance with the specified change in time. After all, as a foreigner in this strange old-new world in which she had elected to live for a while, she would have to conform.

She must have sighed audibly, for the cliché-ridden young man across the aisle suddenly came to life, grinning impudently.

"Poor baby," he said with mock concern. "You're completely discombobulated, aren't you? It's like that when you fly like a bat out of hell from winter into summer. It does things to the old equilibrium — if you know what I mean."

"Yes, I know. The stewardess reminded me. Besides, I wasn't born yesterday," Linda announced defensively.

"No?" He pretended surprise. "Then you know it's one of the hazards of the space age we happen to be living in. But don't let it throw you. It's nothing a couple of day's beddy-bye won't fix. You'll live. We all do."

"I was afraid of that," Linda said, and grinned in spite of her annoyance.

Thus encouraged, Christopher Osborne proceeded to elaborate on a circumstance which was, he declared, at long last being acknowledged by 'head shrinkers' and space authorities the world over: the disorienting effect of the *circadian rhythm* on the human anatomy.

"You travel so fast, you get to wherever you're going before you start — see? Yesterday, today and tomorrow run together till you don't know one from t'other." He looked at Linda pityingly and predicted, "Since this seems to be your first trip, chances are you'll be a hospital case on arrival. Could I offer Your Royal Highness a lift from the airport into the city of Monrovia in my little ol' red ambulance?"

Again Linda refused his offer of a ride, but this time with considerably less hauteur and a tinge of respect. If this character felt half as disoriented as she did, he was doing a fine job of clowning it off. Why, the very words 'hospital' and 'ambulance' — sharp reminders of the past — were like knife thrusts in a conscience that was giving her no peace!

"Thank you," she said, her voice gentler. "It's kind of you to offer me a lift, but my father will be meeting me at the airport."

"Sure of that? Life in this neck of the woods is full of surprise. Nothing is certain but frustration and creeping death."

"Certainly I'm sure. I sent him a cablegram when I changed planes in New York, reminding him I was on my way. It was the last thing I did."

Christopher Osborne shook his head deprecatingly.

"Cripes! That was only last night, ma'am. Meanwhile, you've been zooming along faster than time. Want to bet we didn't zoom past your little ol' cablegram en route?"

"Maybe we did, at that." Linda frowned; then her face brightened. "But that doesn't rule out the letter I wrote a week ago when my reservations came through. Besides, if Father isn't on hand, I'll phone him and wait in a restaurant or somewhere."

Again Chris shook his head. "You may have a long wait my proud beauty. And a dry one. Communication in these parts can be as slow as molasses in January, and the nearest Howard Johnson's is some three thousand miles to the West."

"Oh, well," Linda announced airily, "if worst comes to worst, I can take a taxi."

Her erstwhile companion, chuckling, flashed her a let's-humor-the-child glance, causing her to start resenting him all over again.

"Next thing, I suppose," she flared, "you'll be telling me there are no taxicabs in this part of the world, no telephones. To tell the truth, I've never in all my life met up with such an out-and-out — "

"Stinker's the word, ma'am," he supplied goodnaturedly when she hesitated. "Some of my best friends call me that. My old man says I was born one. Could be he's right for once in his life."

'Stinker' was indeed the word, Linda decided privately, though she'd intended to settle for a less derogatory term: 'wet blanket.' After all, stinkers were made, not born; made by environment, upbringing, as any nurse with an ounce of understanding well knew. Obviously, there was more than met the eye in this mixed-up young man's rebellion against the conventions.

On that benevolent thought, Linda

15

resolved to be patient from here on. But the resolution was short-lived, for the next instant Christopher Osborne, living up to his self-designated role, was saying in a condescending tone that destroyed what little patience she had left:

"Oh, I won't say there are no telephones, but they are mainly in business offices in the city. Today being Sunday, they'll be closed. This is one of those Godfearing communities that pull in the sidewalks on a Saturday night." He waited a moment for that information to sink in, then continued ominously:

"As for taking a taxi — well, it's all of fifty miles, portal to portal, from the airport into the city, through rubber plantations, cobra corrals, tribal villages and stuff. It will cost you fifteen bucks, maybe more. But okay, Miss Astorbilt, If you have that kind of money — "

Linda winced. She did not have that kind of money. If she remembered correctly, she had less than ten dollars left in her purse. And her small savings account — what there was left of it — was, like the nearest Howard Johnson, half a world away. The same fierce pride that had sparked her determination to leave no financial obligation unfulfilled, no loose ends dangling, had prevented her from accepting her father's offer to finance the trip.

Now here it was again: that same stubborn pride, prompting her to lift her chin a lot higher than necessary when Christopher Osborne said with well-meaning solicitude:

"My offer of a lift into the city still holds, Miss Harlan, in case you change your mind. I'll admit I'm a foreigner here myself, but I've been here before, know the ropes, and could show you around. My pleasure," he added quickly when Linda stiffened.

"Thank you again. But I'm sure I can get along under my own power," she said sturdily, though she could not remember when she had been less sure of anything.

Mercifully, Chris Osborne transferred his attention to a second stewardess, to belittle the coffee and fruit juice she was offering him. Couldn't she dig up something stronger in the way of an eye opener? he wanted to know. Couldn't she see he wasn't the pablum type? What kind of an airline was this anyhow? And so on, *ad nauseam* . . .

Thus deprived of a counterirritant, Linda had no choice other than to face her major problem, which had nothing to do with telephones, taxicabs, and fresh upstarts who went around boasting of their indiscretions and heckling their betters. It came to her as a shock that, perversely, she had rather welcomed Chris Osborne's intrusion. It had enabled her to postpone for a while the grueling moment when she would have to take a hard look at herself; answer once and for all time the questions that had been hammering away in the back of her mind ever since she'd announced her decision to give up nursing and start a new life:

Have I made a mistake? Was there no alternative?

All along it had disturbed her to realize that, as she looked back upon the life she was leaving, only the halcyon hours stood out with any clarity. It was as though the heartbreak that had prompted her decision had been dissipated in the rush of preparations, the thrill of flying off to far-away places, the sweet sorrow of saying goodbye to friends and co-workers.

The time had come when she had to examine the whole picture, not just the component parts. She had to face up to the bad along with the good before she would be able to see it in clear perspective.

Above all, she had to settle the argument between a captive heart that demanded escape as a means of self-preservation and an uncompromising conscience that kept repeating, over and over again:

There is no escape from your solemn pledge as a nurse. No matter how fast you run, how far you go, you can never get away from yourself and what you were meant to be.

2

AS she sipped the fruit juice and drank the invigorating coffee, Linda set about the business of taking stock of herself. It occurred to her that she had come a long way from the girl she once was to the girl she was now, and she was not sure she liked the comparison. There was much to remember, more to forget.

The thing to do, of course, was to clean the slate, keeping intact only such memories as would safeguard her against ill-starred romantic entanglements in the future. One thing was certain: She could not possibly build a new life while an accusing conscience stood like a sentinel on guard, and regret for a lost love lay like a hot coal in her heart . . .

A year ago, at twenty, Linda had finished her course in nurse's training, graduating with honors. Full of Florence Nightingale enthusiasm, she had entered service at Boston's Riverview Hospital, her *alma mater*. There she had toiled diligently, loving every minute of it, and beloved — or so she had reason to believe — by the people she worked with and served.

Among her co-workers was attractive, dark-eyed Gregory Arnold, formerly an intern and presently a resident doctor. Together, they had explored the essential facts of life, of sickness, and of death, as applied to their fellow human beings. They had learned how to cope with them according to the best rules of modern medical science.

Later, because their long hours had been virtually the same and their concepts dovetailed, they had shared for a crowded year the triumphs and defeats of their chosen profession. Even the stuffed shirts on the hospital staff agreed that Linda Harlan, nurse, and Gregory Arnold, resident, made an unbeatable team. And more than one grateful patient had been heard to say:

"They belong together; were made for each other and the humanities."

Then, suddenly, it was all over. Like a bubble too fragile for human touch,

Linda's cherished little world had fallen apart in her hands. Propinquity, shared experiences and common ideals had flowered into love.

The shame of it was that it was a one-way attachment, and she herself was both offender and victim. Certainly Greg had said nothing to bring about such a miserable state of affairs. To Linda, it was as though a wanton heart had betrayed her, for surely no girl with any sense of property rights — any sense of self-preservation, for that matter — would lose her head over a man who was practically en route to the altar!

The awareness that Barbara Green, Greg's fiancée, had once been her closest friend made Linda feel all the more despicable. Why, she and Babs had been like sisters through their growing-up years in the village on Cape Cod! For a while, after her mother's death, when Linda was twelve, she had shared Babs' home and family ties. Otherwise, she could not possibly have endured the indescribable loneliness of life without Mother and, later, the shock of Father's remarriage.

Feeling every inch a traitor, Linda

had tried without success to justify this evidence of disloyalty on her part. Under the circumstances, she could not fall back upon the naïve old alibi: "I didn't know he was as good as married."

It was generally known that Gregory Arnold, M.D., and Barbara Green, presently a receptionist in a downtown office building, were planning to be married — and soon. It was also common property — thanks to the allseeing hospital 'grapevine' — that already Greg was buying furniture he could ill afford, for a luxury apartment of Babs' selection in Boston's fashionable Chestnut Hill.

The conviction that Babs' ideas and Greg's ideals were poles apart had done nothing to lessen Linda's feeling of guilt. On the contrary, the mere thought that she would stoop to fault-finding as a means of self-justification was shocking.

Oh, it was true that Babs, always the butterfly, had social ambitions, even delusions of grandeur; whereas Greg was surely destined to be one of those rare human beings: a truly dedicated doctor. But surely, in time, love, the greatest of all alchemies, would bridge the gap between them and they would find happiness together.

Even to herself, Linda had tried to deny her affection for Greg, as if by doing so she could make it go away. She had tried just as diligently to conceal it from others, though she might have realized all along that, to a hospital grapevine, no secret is inviolate. Obviously love, like a skin rash or a cold in the head, was impossible to hide.

As time passed, she'd become increasingly conscious of knowing glances — approving, disapproving, and inevitably pitying. And once a precocious nurse's aide had the temerity to say:

"He's a doll — Dr. Arnold. We're all crazy about him, but it's you he's carrying a torch for. Only he's so wrapped up in his work he doesn't know it yet. Doctors are funny that way. Sharp as a razor about some things, but dumb like a fox about love. They never know what's good for them."

"Nonsense. Greg and I are friends, that's all. He's engaged to a girl I've known all my life."

"Good grief, Miss Harlan, it would be a crying shame if he married that dimwit. Why, every nurse on the staff knows you're in love with each other; thinks you should do something about it. In fact, what they're saying now is — "

"Never mind the gossip!" Linda had protested. "You're all wrong, of course. And I have every intention of doing something. I'm going away — far, far away!"

The words had slipped out, bringing to the forefront a vague thought that Linda had harbored briefly, only to discard it as unworthy, unworkable. For some time she had felt that escape was the only answer to a situation that was rapidly growing intolerable. And yet where to go, how to do it and still save face? What plausible excuse could she give for leaving a job where her work was eminently satisfactory and which represented the culmination of her dreams?

Then, unexpectedly, as if wishing had made it so, she was offered what appeared to be the perfect avenue of escape. It came in a letter from her father, Robert Harlan, whose profession as a mining consultant consigned him to life in far-away places; a nomadic life which Linda, still smarting under the pain of her mother's death and the shock of her father's remarriage, had refused to share. Her face still burned when she recalled the words she'd blurted out in her unreasoning young grief:

"No, thank you, Father. I'd prefer to say here on the Cape with Babs and her family. Later, I'll go to Boston and take up nursing as a career. It's what I've always wanted to do. Oh, don't worry. I'll get along fine, just fine."

Only sixteen at the time of her father's remarriage, Linda had chosen to forget that Mother had been gone for four long years; that Father undoubtedly felt as lonely and as lost as she did.

Many times through the succeeding years, she would have given much to recall those impulsive remarks. But stubborn pride had caused her to reject all overtures, and the breach between father and daughter had widened. Finally, with Linda herself setting the pace, communication had dwindled to an occasional exchange of politely formal letters. That was all.

Therefore the letter urging Linda to 'come join the family in our home-away-from-home' had a dual meaning to the lonely girl whose life was bounded on all sides by hospital walls. Not only did it offer a means of escape from a distressing emotional problem; it opened the way to a reconciliation with the father she'd always adored, had never stopped missing.

Robert Harlan, now living in West Africa with his wife Esther and young stepdaughter Suzy, had pointed up the invitation by adding:

'Why can't we be friends — father and daughter — like we used to be? I have missed you so much, my darling, and I refuse to believe you haven't missed me. Esther, the perennial mother-hen, needs a pretty pigeon to cluck over. Young Suzy, now fifteen and getting a little out of hand, needs the steadying influence of an older sister. The truth is, honey, we all need you — your father most of all . . . '

To Linda, it was a heart-warming appeal, bringing back memories of the old days when Father, Mother and God had constituted her childish Trinity; erasing the fancied grievances of the years in between, and making refusal impossible.

Even so, it had required considerable perjury on her part to sever her hospital connections and still maintain a few shreds of pride. Bombarded by questions which she chose not to answer, she found herself repeating — even rehearsing! — such blasphemies as:

"Well, if you must know, I'm giving up nursing. I've had it. I'm sick to death of oxygen tents, bed pans, fresh interns, fussy doctors, crazy hours, stuffy uniforms. I want to wear pretty clothes like other girls, sleep as late as I like. I want to live, really live, have a little fun for a change . . . "

As she might have expected, nobody believed a word of it. The grapevine consensus was that Linda Harlan — a dedicated nurse, disappointed in love — was slipping off to join the Peace Corps, at great cost to herself. Or perhaps she had decided to make the supreme sacrifice of becoming a medical missionary.

"Otherwise, why would she be traipsing off to Africa, of all places!" her co-workers inquired of one another. Surely, it was agreed, *not* to join a globe-trotting father whom she had not so much as set eyes on in years!

"Africa — don't they still have cannibals there?" a naïve student nurse had queried of an equally naïve associate.

"I wouldn't know about that," was the solemn response. "Could be poor dear Miss Harlan doesn't care if she's eaten alive. It's like that when you've been disappointed in love. Have you seen the newspapers?"

Everyone, from the head surgeon down to the part-time scrubwomen, had seen the newspapers. Or so Linda, badgered by questions and plagued by self-doubts, had concluded. In fact, it seemed more than a mere coincidence that the Boston dailies had carried an announcement of Greg's forthcoming marriage on the very day Linda turned in her resignation. It was as though Fate and the daily press had entered into a conspiracy for the express purpose of humiliating her!

However, the final straw was Greg's wide-eyed, "You can't do this to me, Linda. After all, we're a team. Why, I'd get lost in the assembly line without my favorite teammate. No, pal, you can't do this. I won't let you!"

Had he slapped her face, Linda could not have felt more incensed. Was it possible, as the nurse's aide had implied, that Gregory Arnold, who knew so much about anatomy, did not know the first thing about the deeper areas of the human heart?

"'Favorite teammate,' indeed!" Linda groaned, and wished she had never been born.

* * *

There was a medley of voices, speaking in a babel of tongues, and Linda emerged from her detour into the past to find that the plane had stopped. Passengers from Dakar were coming aboard, dropping such place names as Accra, Abidjan, Lagos, Leopoldville — cities familiar to her only as names in a geography book or a news magazine.

The plane, uncrowded and comparatively quiet through the trans-Atlantic flight, was now a beehive of activity. The aisle was filled with newcomers whose ebony faces mirrored pride of status and whose richly colorful tribal robes marked them as men of distinction in their home bailiwicks. They were talking among themselves, while a flustered stewardess was endeavoring to seat them with due regard for protocol. Apparently there was a misunderstanding as to reservations.

"*Pardon, mademoisells. Permettez moi* — oh, heck, what I mean is, mind if I sit here? There seems to be a *palawa* of some kind going on," a voice said in a mixture of fractured French, uncensored English, and a language which Linda could not identify.

She looked up to see a man of indeterminate age and nationality bending over her. His blond crew cut contrasted sharply with a face deeply tanned by a tropical sun, and she was sure she had never seen such weary blue eyes.

He was wearing conventional Western clothes, well tailored but a bit shiny from many cleanings, and a trifle too roomy for his tall, rangy figure; wearing them with the casual air of one who takes neatness for granted but does not regard clothes as the ultimate measure of man.

He was not handsome, but there was a certain something about him that set him apart from the average modern male. Perhaps it was his hesitant smile, so like that of a boy still unsure of himself. Or his eyes, which were those of a man who has seen a whole lot of life, and not always with the benefit of rose-colored glasses.

When Linda, taken by surprise, did not say anything immediately, he took a deep breath and resorted to a halting combination of words, pantomimes and sound effects as a means of communication.

"Me," he intoned, pointing with a hesitant hand to himself. "Mind?" He indicated the vacant chair at Linda's side, then drawled in a voice as deep-South as hominy grits and black-eyed peas:

"Me no cannibal. Me no eat pretty ladies. Me friendly American — friendly as all get-out."

Linda had to laugh, not so much at his words as the serious expression on his face. "By all means, do sit down," she invited and, impulsively, tacked on the all-American tag line, "before you fall down."

With a sigh of relief, he sank into the chair and deposited a worse-for-wear traveling bag at his feet. "Thank God," he announced fervently, "we speak the same language. We can talk. How lucky can I get?" He flashed Linda a smile so grateful that she was touched. "We can talk," he said again, as if a long-gone guardian angel had reappeared, to maneuver a miracle on his behalf.

Linda returned his smile. "Yes, I'm an American. But I might as well warn you right away that I'm a New Englander and not much of a talker." Then, as an afterthought, because he looked so distressed:

"However, I'm probably one of the world's most dedicated listeners. At least, I've been told that by any number of compulsive talkers. You talk. I'll listen."

His eyes twinkled with amusement, and some of the tiredness went out of them. "You know what? I almost missed this golden opportunity to shoot my mouth off. Just got in from Timbuktu this morning, after traveling on every conveyance known to man, including shank's mare. And am I bushed! Had to run like the devil to catch this plane."

"Timbuktu?" Linda repeated, smiling. "Don't tell me there is such a place? I thought it was only a name, made up by comedians for laughs."

He shook his head in mock reproof. "Yes, Virginia — which isn't your name, I suspect — there *is* a Timbuktu. I've just been there; on a wild goose chase, I might add. I was told I might pick a few recruits for a training program we're setting up in the rain forests of Central Africa . . . " He broke off to say, by way of introduction:

"My name is Paul Raymond — Doc for short. Not that it means anything — not yet. Yours?"

"My name is Linda Harlan. It doesn't mean anything either — never will."

He nodded and said matter-of-factly, "No, I guess it won't. You'll probably be changing it any day. Pretty girls, I've noticed, are allergic to single harness."

Linda smiled noncommittally and let it go at that.

The plane became airborne, and a stewardess, bringing breakfast trays, assured them that they would have plenty of time for leisurely eating before reaching Monrovia. While they ate, Paul Raymond, apparently hungrier for conversation than food, did most of the talking; Linda, the listening, as she'd promised. Meanwhile, Christopher Osborne, except for an occasional glance across the aisle, had the grace to mind his own business.

As she listened, Linda found herself growing increasingly interested in a story that, in some respects, was peculiarly like her own.

Born and brought up in a small Alabama town, Paul Raymond had gone to Philadelphia, full of dreams about becoming a doctor and curing the world of whatever ailed it — "which was just about everything, from warts to war, in my harebrained opinion," he confessed. "However, I would fix it, I assured myself, and good. I was that confident."

He had worked his way through pre-med and medical schools; finished his internship at a name hospital in the City of Brotherly Love, and was in line for a residency . . .

"Then something happened," he confided, and closed his lips against further disclosure. "We'll just say I lost my favorite marble. Anyhow, I decided to get away from it all. Talked my way into the Peace Corps and came as far off as possible."

Linda, aware that his eyes had grown old again and that his boyish grin was no longer in evidence, did not press him for details. She needed no sixth sense to tell her that the circumstance which had prompted Dr. Paul Raymond to give up his career was no trivial thing. She had a strong feeling that his motivation was even greater than hers, and somehow it shamed her.

"Oh, so you're a Peace Corps volunteer? Why, that's wonderful!" she exclaimed, groping for a lighter note. "You don't look the type," she bantered. "Where's your beard, long hair, blue jeans? I was under the impression they were mostly young activists — you know, full of vim, vigor and protest."

Paul Raymond was not amused. "Bless them. They're doing a fine job, often against odds." He waited a moment, then answered Linda's question:

"I *was* a Peace Corps volunteer, but I'm not any more. I dug ditches, built roads, taught school, knowing all the time I was a misfit. I was only tilting at windmills."

"Then what?" Linda prompted, though she felt she'd already guessed the answer.

"Well, I shaved off my beard, got a crew cut, and returned to my first love — my only love *now*: medical research." He was smiling again, and his eyes had lost their tired look. "It was high time I got back into the groove. I'm pushing thirty-one. There's a whole lot to be done, so I haven't too much time."

Linda could not suppress a smile, as he took a deep breath and continued: "Funny thing about the medical profession. Once you get into any phase of it, you're a gone goslin'. The self you have to live with won't let you fold up and quit."

Linda averted her face, not wanting

him to see the quick flush that mantled her cheeks. She had an uncomfortable feeling that this medicine man was reading her mind. He must have misinterpreted her action, for he stiffened and said:

"Am I boring you, Miss Harlan? Looks like I'm one of those compulsive talkers you mentioned a while ago. Sorry. It isn't often I have such a patient listener."

"Of course I'm not bored." Linda, turning to face him, spoke with genuine enthusiasm. "I'm listening because I'm interested. Go on, please. Tell me more. What's happening with you now?"

Obligingly, Dr. Paul Raymond gave a brief résumé of his current activities. Thanks to a modest grant from a philanthropic group of Americans, he and an older doctor were operating a medical center and health clinic in the rain forests of Central Africa. He himself was also doing research on endemic diseases, presently concentrating on malaria, which he described as "Enemy Number One of the Tropics."

"Of course, I don't fancy myself a budding Schweitzer," he admitted. "But I will say that I am doing a pretty fair job, considering the frustrations, limited facilities and the raw talent we have to work with."

He digressed here to point out the critical shortage of medical personnel in that part of the world. In the whole Continent, he explained, the overall average was less than two doctors to every twenty thousand people — "not counting witch doctors, of course." It would take years of specialized training to reach even a modest coverage.

"We're training our own help at the clinic," he went on to say. "Operating a small pre-med school, in fact. I'm stopping off in Monrovia a few days, scouting for recruits, before shoving off for the bush."

"How are you fixed for nurses — any R.N.'s?" Linda bit her lip in vexation, realizing too late that her interest was getting out of bounds.

"Nurses, did you say?" Paul Raymond flashed his boyish grin. "Are you kidding? Lady, if I ever set eyes on an R.N., I'll kidnap her. I might even be persuaded to marry her. Seen any good nurses lately?"

"Scads of them," Linda said, laughing.

"I still think you're kidding. Even in the States, I'm told, they're scarce enough. Really good ones, I mean."

"You've been misinformed, Dr. Raymond," Linda exclaimed. "Why, at Riverview in Boston, where I trained and worked, the nurses are wonderful," she raced on, her enthusiasm getting the better of her. "When you're on the staff there, you've got to be better than good. You never know what emergencies — "

"Whoa there!" he broke in. "Don't tell me you're a nurse? How dumb can I get? I should have recognized the symptoms: patience, fortitude, interest in medical shop talk." He bent over and peered at the identification tag on Linda's traveling bag. "So you're bound for Monrovia, are you, Nurse Harlan?"

"I *was* a nurse, but I'm not any more. I've given it up for keeps," Linda stammered, feeling trapped. She waited for the recriminations that would surely follow. But Paul Raymond, M.D., simply smiled and said complacently:

"Something tells me we've still got a whole lot to talk about, young lady. Now, let's have your Monrovia address." With the assurance of one who brooks no refusal, he took pencil and notebook from his jacket pocket and held them in readiness.

Not wanting to hurt him, Linda repeated the address and phone number her father had sent, but resolved to be 'out' when Paul Raymond called.

"Good girl. I'll see you soon," he commented as he wrote.

Not if she had anything to say about it, Linda promised herself. It was hard enough to wrestle with an uncompromising conscience. It would be still harder to cope with the dangerously persuasive arguments of a crusading medicine man who had all the potentials of a mind reader!

3

AS Christopher Osborne had predicted, Linda's father was not waiting at the airport. And so she was obliged to eat crow sooner than she'd anticipated, much sooner, she felt, than Fate had a right to demand of a girl whose human rights surely included the first law of life: self-preservation.

On the field, behind the barrier, she had looked in vain for the welcoming face of her father. Paul Raymond, M.D., after a gay "So long for now, Nurse Harlan; see you soon," had gone off with friends who had come to meet him. Chris Osborne, so omnipresent earlier, was conspicuous only by his absence.

By some minor miracle, Linda had managed to clear Customs, grateful that her heavier luggage was being sent by air freight. Then, not knowing what else to do, she had come into the lounge — to wait, to think what to do.

As she sat watching people of many

races saying hail or farewell in divers languages, she had plenty of time to think. Too much time, in fact. With merciless precision, her thoughts moved out of the disturbing past into the equally disturbing present. Questions flooded her mind.

Was it possible that Father, bogged down with business problems, had overlooked the fact that this was the day scheduled for her arrival? Or, what was even worse, was he so wrapped up in his second family that he'd forgotten his first-born ever existed? Was his invitation to 'come join the family' nothing more than a brush-off, an easy way of saying goodbye?

Had she, Linda, erred in responding so wholeheartedly, so quickly? Had she burned her bridges too soon?

How ridiculous can you get? she admonished herself. He's been delayed, of course. Evidently Chris Osborne, for all his tomfoolery, had been right about one thing: the cablegram had not arrived. But the letter, written two weeks ago, undoubtedly had been received in good time. Oh, Father would show up eventually!

Now the crowd was thinning out, and soon she would be the sole occupant of a room which was growing more formidable by the minute. Hesitantly she summoned a uniformed African attendant and inquired by way of carefully articulated one-syllable words, aided by gestures, the whereabouts of a public telephone.

"That is," she blurted, thinking aloud in her frustration, "if there is such a contraption in this never-never spot."

"There is indeed such a contraption, missy," the man announced in the carefully precise English which Linda was to learn later was the official language of modern Liberia. He did not add, "You do not need to talk down to me," but the hurt look on his dark face did not escape her.

"But this is the Lord's Day," he declared, pointing up another aspect of Liberian life: a profound respect for the religion upon which the Republic was built. "Business places do not remain open, and few private homes are equipped with telephones as yet."

With the deference of a polite host

presenting the keys of the city to a respected but not too bright guest, he indicated a telephone on a counter at the far end of the lounge, bowed courteously and went on his way.

I probably won't know how to use the darn thing, being only a bungling foreigner, Linda thought in a sudden rush of humility. Nevertheless, she picked up the instrument and dialed several times. When there was no answer, she returned to her seat, feeling hopelessly inadequate.

Then panic overtook her and, to her dismay, she burst into tears. She could not remember when, if ever, she had felt so completely alone, so unwanted, so far away from home . . .

"Oh, so here you are, Cinderella! Big as life but not half so sassy. What's the matter — lost your slipper? Me — I've been out inspecting my new scooter, a welcome-prodigal gift from the old man. Who says delinquency doesn't pay?"

Recognizing the voice of Chris Osborne, Linda squeezed back the tears as best she could and managed to bestow a watery smile upon her savior-came-lately, who was advancing toward her in the now deserted waiting room.

Christopher Osborne, who had done considerable knocking around in his twenty-three ill-spent years, was not deceived. He returned her smile with a commiserating glance and crowded his long, athletic body into the seat beside her.

"Poor chickadee," he crooned, pulling an unreasonably long face. "You're crying. What happened? Bigbad wolf on the choo-choo plane give you a rough time? I had an eye on him. Never trusted guys with non-stop tongues and cotton-pickin' hairdos."

"If you're talking about Dr. Paul Raymond — and I suppose you are — he certainly didn't give me a hard time. I've never met a more interesting man. He's dedicated — and I do mean dedicated. And I am not crying," Linda denied, choking back a sob.

"You are so crying. Practically bawling." Taking a handkerchief from his breast pocket, Chris made a great show of mopping Linda's face, then dabbed at his own eyes. "Now you've got me doing

46

it, too. Want to tell Chris what's digging you? Whatever it is, it can't be as bad as you think. Nothing's worth a gorgeous girl's tears."

He put an arm around her, and Linda let it stay there a moment, torn between a need to confess her predicament in full and a diminishing desire to save face. Somehow it was comforting to have a man around — even a scapegrace — to assure her that nothing was so bad it couldn't be worse. Then pride took over and she released herself.

He took her withdrawal in stride. "Never mind. You don't need to tell me. Your pappy didn't get the cablegram. I could say I told you so, only I'm too much of a gentleman to strike a lady when she's already down in the dumps."

He laughed at the absurd remark, and Linda found herself laughing with him. There was a kind of infectious gayety about this uninhibited young man that gave her a strange sense of release, now that she was seeing him in the role of rescuer rather than heckler. At least he did not make her feel guilty, chained to the past, as Paul Raymond had done. Or bound by ties of loyalty and misplaced affection, as had been the case with Gregory Arnold. In any case, she reasoned, it was better to laugh than to cry.

Actually, she decided, Chris Osborne could be fun — harmless fun, too. He was, she supposed, a typical exponent of the carefree life she had never known, soon would know. Undoubtedly she would be meeting more of his kind in the months ahead; must learn how to laugh at their corny jokes and to play along with them.

Abruptly, Chris rose to his feet, picked up Linda's bags and caught her arm. "On your toes, slowpoke!" he commanded. "It's time we were on our way to the fleshpots of Monrovia. With luck, we should be there within the half-hour."

"But — " Linda demurred, wishing he would be less highhanded.

"No buts about it, sugar-bun. Your carriage awaits without — without hosses, I might add. She doesn't need hosses — not that beautiful heap. She's got more get-up-and-go of her own than all the prize livestock in Texas."

"You don't have to twist my arm, cowpoke," Linda retorted, meeting his nonsense halfway. "I'll go quietly."

Laughing, she allowed herself to be piloted out of the air-conditioned lounge into the sizzling sunlight of a West African mid-morning. It seemed incredible that only yesterday, in Boston, she'd been practically whipped to pieces by a violent early-November wind, accompanied by a premature sleet storm. Her erstwhile Sir Galahad must have sensed her thoughts, for he said:

"Hot as you-know-where, isn't it? But keep smiling, ma'am. Don't forget there's a long, rugged winter ahead in New England. Just think how lucky you are to be here and to have me and my little ol' red ambulance at your disposal."

"You're impossible, Chris Osborne," Linda giggled, caught up by his infectious light-heartedness.

★ ★ ★

Christopher Osborne's 'little ol' ambulance' was a de luxe fire-engine red racing car. Obviously, it was brand-new and

49

equipped with all the modern gadgetry that money could buy. Chris released Linda's arm long enough to indicate with a grandiose gesture the sleek vehicle and to say, quite unnecessarily:

"See? She's got everything — and I do mean everything."

Linda nodded. "Yes — except perhaps a roof to keep off this blistering sun."

"Racing cars don't have roofs, ma'am," Chris retorted indulgently, as if Linda did not know. "Sorry. If I'd known you were coming, I'd have fetched an umbrella."

Linda nodded again, smiling. The racer was, she reflected, the perfect toy for a pampered playboy who had money in his wallet, time on his hands, and nothing but fun on his mind. It could also — she cringed at the thought — be an instrument of death in the hands of a young daredevil who regarded the world as his playground, the world's highways as his personal race track!

She was heartened to see a liveried black chauffeur standing at attention beside the elegant vehicle. Nevertheless, she could not imagine how Chris Osborne expected three adults, not to speak of an assortment of luggage — his and hers — to fit into the limited space. Chris settled that question immediately.

"That's all for now, Mac," he told the elderly colored chauffeur, whose name, quite obviously, was not Mac. "You can take my bags and, if you'll run like the devil, maybe you can get a lift back on a luggage truck. I'm taking over the racer."

"Yes, sir, boss. As you wish," the man said with the stolidity of one accustomed to the swashbuckling young Texan's highhandedness. "But I thought I was supposed to — "

"You were supposed to deliver. Period. Now, get the lead out of your feet and get going."

Without another word, the man picked up Chris' bags and got going.

"The old fellow says this baby can make ninety a minute without turning a hair," Chris told Linda, indicating the car. "She's got to do better — or else. Now, anchor your curls and hop in. In a minute we'll be burning the wind."

"Do you think you should — drive, I mean?" Linda protested, disturbed by his whirlwind proclivities and recalling his earlier remarks about the ill effects of the *circadian rhythm*. "Sure you feel all right? Don't forget you're discombobulated."

He looked at her accusingly, as though she'd invented the outlandish word. "What do you mean, do I feel all right? Never felt better. I've got to get the feel of this baby, get my hands on the wheel. If she doesn't do what she's supposed to do, my old man can send her right back to France where she came from. I have no intention of being earmarked as just another American sucker. No-siree!"

When Linda did not say anything, his face registered surprise. "Don't tell me you're scared? I never dreamed there were gals of the chicken persuasion still floating around."

"I am *not* the chicken type," Linda retorted stiffly. "As a hospital nurse, I've lived through more scarestories than you could ever dream up. I have yet to be afraid of anything reasonable."

"Oh." Chris made a sour face and addressed the world at large. "Can you tie that? The lady thinks I'm unreasonable, can't drive a car. Me — Chris Osborne, who was born to a four-car garage with a steering wheel in my hand. Shucks — I've been fiddling around with motors ever since I was knee-high to a jackrabbit!"

Linda, though apprehensive, allowed herself and her two pieces of hand luggage to be crowded into the compact luxury car. Maybe she was taking a long chance, she reflected. However, her one alternative was to take out, lickety-split, after the dispossessed chauffeur, and 'run like the devil' in the vague hope of catching a ride on a luggage truck.

Of one thing she was certain: she could not possibly face the ordeal of hitchhiking for fifty long miles through what Chris Osborne had described as 'cobra corrals, tribal villages, rubber plantations and stuff.' The chances were that he was only trying to shock her. But how was she, a stranger in a strange land, to know?

Under the circumstances, she could no more argue with a man who admittedly knew the ropes than she could quarrel with a kindly Fate that had spared her the indignity of walking!

"So far, so good," Chris commented

as he tooled the racer out of the parking area onto the highway. "She starts off like a breeze. Now, we'll see how she performs in the speed department. I aim to gun her up to the limit," he promised, and proceeded to do just that.

* * *

Even if she lived to a ripe old age, which seemed most unlikely at the time, Linda was sure she would never forget the wild ride from Robertsfield into the city of Monrovia. However, if Chris Osborne chose to play Russian roulette with a high-powered racer, there was nothing she could do about it, she supposed. He was the man in the driver's seat, while she was only the helpless by-sitter.

Responsive to its master's every touch, the little car put on an extraordinary performance. Even Chris appeared satisfied. Soon his grin became a facial fixture, as he pressed hard, harder, on the accelerator.

Alarmed, Linda tore her eyes away from the climbing speedometer. Clutching at her wind-blown hair and trying desperately to dismiss the growing conviction that she was being betrayed by a fellow-American and roasted alive by an African sun, she managed finally to concentrate on the passing panorama.

She caught brief glimpses of great forests whose tapped trees identified them as part of the vast Firestone Rubber Plantation; fleeting views of neat company houses, made of fieldstone and stucco, enhanced by flowering shrubs. She also observed many thatched huts, huddling together as if seeking companionship.

"Bugaboo huts, many of them," Chris offered, adding by way of explanation that the mud-bricks forming their walls were made of 'bugaboo,' as the giant ant hills along the way were called.

Linda was conscious of many faces: smiling ebony faces that bespoke friendly curiosity; happy faces that registered contentment, even pride in their modest surroundings. It was, she reflected, a thought-provoking sight in a world crawling with people who had everything — but never enough.

Every now and then the racing car would whizz past a roadside pavilion whose open front revealed all manner of decorative articles, from intricately woven baskets to painted gourds and incredibly long festoons of beads.

"They look fascinating, what little I can see of them," Linda told Chris. "If only you'd slow up a bit — "

He did not slow up, though he did return to sanity long enough to explain that the articles on display included such African artifacts as devils' masks, tribal drums, and fertility dolls carved from native wood.

The 'beads,' he said, were polished seed from the cha-cha tree, gathered and strung by native women and small children as a source of income. The 'fertility dolls' were what the name implied, guaranteeing a bumper baby crop. Sometimes they were buried in rice paddies, to insure a bountiful harvest — and often, in the event of failure, they were dug up and given welldeserved beatings.

"Some day," Chris promised, "we'll take a spin out here and you can have yourself a ball game, buying stuff for all your friends. At your own price, too.

That is, if you know how to bargain."

"That is, if I live that long," Linda corrected him. "But I never bargain, especially with people who are trying to earn an honest living. If I can't afford a thing, I just do without it."

"Wow! That's trimming me down to size."

All along the way there were pedestrians, men dressed in their Sunday best, many of them carrying colorful umbrellas to ward off the November sun; women wearing bright costumes, which were known as 'lappas,' Chris remarked in passing. Some of the women also wore babies, strapped to their backs. Others, unencumbered, were swinging along with the easy grace that professional models strive for and do not always achieve.

A few of the younger women wore costumes whose patterned fabrics portrayed with lifelike fidelity the countenances of such personages as Abraham Lincoln, John F. Kennedy, or their own revered President; each pictured face changing expression with the wearer's every movement. Linda, moved by what she felt was a touching evidence of affection for their heroes, living or dead, was shocked to hear Chris say:

"Looks like there is something to be said for broads with broad bottoms — huh?"

"You should be ashamed of yourself, Chris Osborne," she exclaimed. "If you had the slightest degree of social consciousness, you'd know that what you're seeing now is patriotism in motion."

"You don't say?" Chris chortled, and Linda lapsed into a disdainful silence.

Among the roadside spectators, there were many children who stopped whatever they were doing to stare in wide-eyed wonder as the red racer whizzed by. And more than one protesting dog, chancing sudden death, dashed forward to intercept the speeding monster. Each time, with a deft turn of the wheel, Chris managed to avoid hitting the intrepid animal. There was no gainsaying the fact that he was an expert driver.

Finally, when the racer all but grazed a 'mammy wagon' which was being readied for tomorrow's trip to the market, Linda could remain silent no longer.

"*Must* you keep on playing cowboy-on-a-binge?" she demanded. "Isn't there a speed law or something?"

Chris shrugged, as much as to say that laws were made to be broken; that he, Christopher Osborne the Second, was a law unto himself.

"Today's Sunday," he announced calmly. "All good lawmen are in church. If they aren't, they ought to be."

Linda tried another approach. "Maybe you don't care what happens to you, or how many people you maim. But I do. And I'd hate to wind up in jail. My father would disown me, as he should."

Chris took a hand off the wheel long enough to rub thumb and forefinger together, making the money sign. "You won't wind up in jail, and I'm not likely to be hung for giving my own car a tryout. I'll admit they're pretty fond of law and order hereabouts. My old man warned me. But I have yet to meet up with a place where the long green doesn't talk. It's the universal language."

Linda took a deep breath and said what was actually on her mind. "Now I know how the term 'ugly American' got started. It was invented for people like you; people who have no regard for human rights — except their own. I don't wonder the whole world is starting to hate us."

For the first time her words seemed to register. Chris took his foot off the accelerator, slowing the car to a normal rate of speed, and said in the tone of one who has been cruelly misjudged:

"You don't like me one little bit, do you, ma'am? Nobody ever questioned my social consciousness before. Matter of fact, you hate me. I was sort of hoping you wouldn't."

"I don't hate anybody."

"Seems I got started off on the wrong foot." He shook his head dolefully and reduced the car's speed to what was virtually a snail's pace. "My mistake. I should have handed you the usual malarkey, telling you only the best about myself and letting you find out the ugly truth for yourself. That's the customary routine. Truth is, I'm not such a bad guy at heart."

Disarmed by this sudden about-face, Linda was at a loss for something to say.

Finally, still groping for suitable words, she took refuge in the commonplace, quoting the old lines:

"'There's so much good in the worst of us, so much bad in the best of us, it scarcely behooves any of us to talk about the rest of us.'"

"Thank you. That takes a load off my mind," Chris said, and looked as though he meant it.

"I'm sure you have any number of good qualities," Linda murmured, bending over backward in a determination to be fair. "Of course," she amended in the interest of truth, "you do like to shock people, but that seems to be the thing nowadays. It's a kind of emotional sickness, I suppose. And it's impossible to know whether you're joking or serious."

"I'm serious right now," Chris avowed. "Who says I'm sick? And who says I have no regard for human rights? Shucks — you should have seen me marching in freedom parades last summer. Me — a born Texan! And I've carried protest placards on more campuses than you could ever shake a stick at."

Linda managed not to smile. It

occurred to her that, for a person who marched in freedom parades, Chris Osborne had been most inconsiderate of his colored chauffeur. And his blithe disregard for the rights of pedestrians along their own highway was nothing short of shameful. However, inconsistency was a human failing; she herself could not claim immunity. On that thought she said impulsively:

"You could be rehabilitated, you know. It's not too late to back up and start over again. I could say you were hopeless. But with all the good qualities you surely must have — "

Her reward was a grateful smile and an eager, "Mind taking on the job, ma'am? You'll never find a more obliging patient. And just look what you'd be doing for a fouled-up world."

Linda did not answer at once. She had a vague feeling that she was still being heckled. Nevertheless, here was a challenge, not only to her skill as a nurse but also to her finer instincts as a human being. True, it involved a tremendous undertaking. But it might — just *might* — ease her conscience, give her something constructive to do while she went about the more complicated task of rehabilitating herself.

Interpreting her silence as agreement and being a stranger to opposition of any sort, Chris grinned and said with returning lightheartedness:

"When does the noble experiment start, ma'am? As of now?"

"Certainly not," Linda retorted. "How premature can you get? There are a lot of things to be taken into consideration. In the first place, I don't like — "

He reached over and placed a finger on her lips. "No need to say it, honey-bun. You don't like my hair-do. Tomorrow, I'm getting one of those cotton-pickin' crew cuts, like that sawbones you were cozying up to on the plane. That's a promise. So why not start on Operation Rehabilitation right now?"

4

AS the racing car moved discreetly through the attractive suburbs and the tree-lined streets of the city, Chris was strangely silent. There was no more heckling, no further attempts to shock, no daredevil driving whatsoever. He appeared to have taken on a new personality, which included such cardinal virtues as humility and regard for the rights of his fellow man.

But was it real? Linda wondered. Did Christopher Osborne — as was remotely possible — actually have hidden qualities worthy of exploration, encouragement? Or was he pulling a fast one?

She tried to draw him out by expressing her delight over a city whose beauty and modernity far exceeded her expectations.

"Right now, back in Boston, the slush from yesterdays freak sleet-storm is probably shoe-mouth deep," she exaggerated. "But it's June in November here. The trees are a living green, and

64

there are flowers everywhere. Why, this is like a dream city, come alive!"

Chris nodded. "It *is* a dream city, come to life." With unwonted solemnity, he proceeded to relate the story of a handful of former Negro slaves who, almost a century and a half ago, had come to Africa from America with the dream of establishing a home, a free state, for themselves and their descendants. Despite privations and heartbreaking setbacks, they had pulled themselves up by the bootstraps and survived. The ultimate result of their labors was a proud Republic, the oldest in Africa, and a thriving city which was rapidly becoming the pride of the West African Riviera.

"They named the capital city Monrovia, after one of our Presidents, James Monroe, as a gesture of appreciation and friendliness," Chris finished, and again fell silent.

"Please go on," Linda urged. The story was not new to her, the buildings of the Republic of Liberia being a matter of history. But now she was seeing a new side of the enigmatic Chris Osborne and was impressed — though only for clinical reasons, she assured herself.

He shrugged, as if washing his hands of the whole thing, including the girl sitting beside him. "That's all there is, ma'am; there isn't any more. Anyhow, here we are, in Monrovia. Where do you want to go?"

"My father, Robert Harlan, lives on Mamba Point, wherever that is." Linda began to fumble in her purse for the street address. For some reason, she felt ill at ease. It seemed to her that Chris Osborne's newly acquired humility was even more disconcerting than his heckling.

"Never mind looking, Miss Diogenes. Anybody around there can tell us. Mamba Point happens to be where a whole slue of us ugly-rich Americans live, so we stick out like sore thumbs. It's named after the mamba, the tree cobra, which might have a double meaning, though I wouldn't know about that, being the ugliest one of them all."

As he spoke, Chris turned on his mocking grin, and Linda secretly welcomed it back. "Mamba Point, here comes Miss

Universe!" he chortled. "Pull in your snakes, drag out the red carpet, and put the big pot in the little one. She rates all of that and more."

★ ★ ★

Mamba Point is one of the choice beauty spots in the picturesque city of Monrovia. Rising to a height of some three hundred feet, it is bounded on two sides by the white-crested Atlantic. On the third side, it looks down with affection upon a growing metropolis, rich in tradition, unique in history; a city born of dreams, nurtured by the blood, sweat and tears — and the prayers — of a people who earned freedom the hard way and whose descendants cherish it accordingly. Regardless of Chris Osborne's unflattering pronouncement, the white Americans who live there step lightly, knowing they are walking on dreams.

As the racing car proceeded effortlessly up the incline that led to The Point, Chris indicated with the wave of a hand an ultramodern structure that seemed to dominate the scene ahead.

"That handsome heap," he explained, "is the Intercontinental Hotel, my old man's home-away-from-home, for now. My home, too, I suppose, till he decides he doesn't like the way I trim my nails." He opened his lips to say more, then shut them just as quickly.

Taking the cue, Linda returned the conversation to the hotel. "It's fabulous. I suppose it's got everything, too," she teased.

Yes, he admitted, the Intercontinental had everything — "plus a perfumed swimming pool and a smoother-than-glass dance floor." He added:

"One of these evenings, when you get back on the ball, we'll put on our glad rags and show the local yokels how to cut a rug the good ol' American way."

Linda flinched at the bigotry implied in his words. But he's *trying*, she told herself firmly, resolved to give Chris the benefit of any reasonable doubt.

They drove past the American Embassy, easily identifiable by Old Glory floating so gallantly against an alien blue sky that Linda felt a mist of tears in her eyes, and a feeling of nostalgia swept over her. Presently they entered a compound whose snow-white walls were all but obscured by a curtain of bougainvillea and pink hibiscus, and whose enchanting villas might easily have been part of a stage setting.

Chris brought the car to a stop in front of the prettiest villa of them all. Perched on a bluff and with a whole ocean for a backyard, it nestled in a garden of flowering trees and lush tropical shrubs, awaiting its turn to be admired.

A young girl stood on the terrace, staring out toward the ocean, a miniature gray poodle in her arms. A white-uniformed black man, obviously a servant, hovered nearby, as though to shield her from any untoward contact with a commonplace world.

"Hi there, beautiful dreamer!" Chris bellowed in a voice that must have been heard all the way to the airport. "Mind coming down off Cloud Nine long enough to tell a couple of mere human beings if a character name of Robert Harlan lives any place around here?"

Despite Chris' extravagant salutation, the girl was not beautiful, Linda observed; yet she might have been pretty in a gamine sort of way, were it not for the sullen look in her blue eyes and the expression of discontent that wreathed her small mouth. She was wearing stretch pants and a hug-me-tight overblouse that accented the curves of blossoming young womanhood, while her long blonde hair, blown this way and that by a brisk ocean breeze, gave her the unkempt appearance of a careless child.

Upon hearing Chris' voice, she turned to look at him, and a heart-shaped face remarkable mainly for its sullen discontent was transformed into one of radiant charm. Either she did not see Linda or chose not to do so. Handing the poodle over to the manservant, she moved with self-conscious grace toward the car.

"I am sorry, very sorry," she told Chris in a formal little voice that did not match up with the rest of her. "Did you ask something?"

Chris repeated the question in a less condescending tone, adding: "Neat pad you've got here, ma'am."

"*This* is the residence of Mr. Robert Harlan," the girl said. "I am his daughter — his stepdaughter, I mean."

"How come I've never seen you before?" Chris queried after a swift but rather thorough appraisal of the girl's feminine charms. "I was rattling around here most of last winter."

Her face flushed prettily. "Oh, I was here. Only you didn't see me, I guess. Anyhow, I saw you, Mr. Osborne."

"I must have been blind or something," Chris said, turning on the charm.

The girl's flush deepened. "Oh, no, I wouldn't say that. It was just that I was in school most of the time. My name is — "

"Wait a minute, Goldilocks!" Chris exclaimed with an elaborate show of surprise. "Don't tell me. Let me guess. You're cute little ol' Suzy, grown up. Well, shut my mouth and call me Batman!"

The girl giggled. "Yes, Mr. Osborne, I'm Suzy," she said in a voice so coy that Linda squirmed and Chris looked abashed.

Conscious of the awkwardness of the situation, Linda decided to break it up. "And I'm Linda, your sister," she said, allowing Chris to help her out of the car.

There was a painful moment of silence while Suzy struggled for poise. Then, lifting a smooth cheek for Linda's kiss, she clasped her hands in a childish gesture of distress and murmured a grown-up, if slightly dubious, apology:

"Yes, of course. You're Linda, my stepsister. Please forgive me. I never dreamed it was you in the car. I'm so sorry. If only we'd known you were coming today — "

It was her turn to apologize, Linda supposed. "It's probably my fault, dear. I sent a cablegram, but not soon enough maybe. But I did write a letter earlier, giving my plans."

"You must have sent it sea mail, not realizing it takes ages. But then, a lot of people have no conception of distance," Suzy said, her courteous manner offsetting to some extent the criticism implied in her words.

"It's really wicked there's no one here

to welcome you but me," she continued. "Robert, my stepfather, is in Ghana on a business trip. And Esther, my mother, is at the Intercontinental, overseeing a charity bazaar. Otherwise they'd have met you at Robertsfield. They'll feel dreadful, really crushed."

"It's all right, cutie-pie. I'm here, safe and sound, all in one piece — thanks to our friend Chris, who gave me a lift."

Suzy's response was a stiffly polite, "That was marvelous of Mr. Osborne, considering it was *our* responsibility to get you here."

"My pleasure," Chris inserted, rising to the occasion.

Suzy's lips parted in a deprecating smile. "You *would* say that, naturally," she told Chris, "though you probably had scads of plans of your own."

Linda, more than a little nonplussed by this odd combination of childish naïveté and adult sophistication that was her young stepsister, had not meant to talk down to the girl. She had heard of youngsters, bemused by the superficial glamour of overseas living, who were neither adults nor children. Evidently

Suzy was one of these. She, Linda, would have to move carefully; she did not want to hurt this child-woman.

"But don't think you aren't welcome," Suzy was saying with the stilted civility of one repeating a carefully rehearsed speech. "We're going to love having you here, and we hope you'll like us and have fun. We'll hate ourselves if you don't."

A second manservant appeared, seemingly out of nowhere, and took Linda's bags. Then Suzy, having fulfilled her duty as hostess *pro tem*, returned her attention to Chris.

"I'm desolate because I can't invite you in for a drink or something, Mr. Osborne," she caroled. "But I'm sure you wouldn't want kid stuff like coke or tonic, and that's all I'm allowed to serve." She made a sour face, then smiled ever so sweetly. "If only my mother and stepfather were at home — "

"Think nothing of it, young lady. I never drink anything stronger than bourbon." Chris got back into the car and turned on the ignition. "Now I'd better shove off. It's time I got reacquainted with my own never-lovin'

74

family." He tossed Linda a quick wink, which she ignored. "So long, dolls; I'm off to the Osborne palawa hut."

"You'll come back, won't you?" Suzy pleaded. "I'm sure my mother and stepfather will want to thank you for your kindness to Linda — "

"Sure thing. I'll be back. Wild hosses couldn't keep me away from two such de-lovely young ladies."

"Soon? *Very* soon?"

"Why not?" Chris, looking somewhat disconcerted, as though suddenly realizing he was getting involved, assumed a paternal attitude. "If you're a good child and keep your nose clean, I might take you for a spin out to the airport and back one of these fine days."

"Oh, *would* you!" Suzy squealed in schoolgirlish delight. "I've never seen such a luscious car. It's cool, cool, cool!"

Chris' reaction was a curious blend of pride and masculine caution. Young Suzy, in her pseudo-sophistication, had located the spot where his heart lived: his newest and most treasured possession, the de luxe red racer.

"You can say that again, Sis," he told Suzy. "And if you're super-good, I might even be persuaded to give you a turn at the wheel. Know how to drive?"

"I could learn," the girl announced breathlessly. "After all, I'm not just a child, as *some* people seem to think. Next year I'll be sixteen, going on seventeen."

"You don't say? That practically makes you an old cowhand, doesn't it?"

He's baiting her, the stinker, Linda told herself angrily. How did I ever get the idea he was worth rehabilitating? It must have been the nurse syndrome, a hangover from the Boston hospital days.

Impaling the helpless young man with a malevolent glance, she managed to convey with her eyes a scathing indictment that no proper Bostonian would dream of putting into words. The message must have registered with considerable impact; or, possibly, Chris decided he was sticking his neck out too far.

In any case, he lifted a hand in salute. Then, pausing only to shout a cavalier, "'Bye for now, dolls," he gunned the racer and tore out of the compound, as if all the evil spirits of African folklore were in hot pursuit . . .

"He's a little unrestrained, but he's a doll if ever there was one," Suzy murmured as she walked with Linda along the flagstones that led to the steps of the villa. "I've never seen such long eyelashes on a man, or such a divine car. I'm getting goose pimples all over, just thinking about riding in it."

Linda tried to divert the conversation by remarking on the charm of the villa and its surroundings; her delight in being there as a member of the family. But it was no use. Suzy was back on Cloud Nine, so nothing mundane could touch her.

"Of course," Suzy sighed presently, "Robert — your father, that is — will disapprove of his hair-do. But I think it's cute. I love the way it curls up around his ears, though he probably hates that. I'd adore getting my hands on it — you know, training it."

Linda stole a cautious glance at the girl, hoping to see a bantering smile that might offset the absurd remarks. But no, Suzy was serious, deadly serious. Conscious of the delicacy of the situation, Linda searched her mind for a comment that would neither condemn nor condone, finally coming up with:

"You don't need to worry about Father, honey. Chris knows I don't like long hair on a man, either, so he's getting a crew cut tomorrow. He promised."

Suzy stiffened and returned to earth with an alacrity that must have disassembled the pink cloud she'd been riding on. "Oh," she said in a tight little voice. "So you've already put the Indian sign on Mr. Osborne. I might have expected that."

"Nonsense. Now you really *are* being a child." Linda sensed she'd said the wrong thing, but somehow she could not stop herself. "Why, I never set eyes on that stinker before last night. As far as I'm concerned, he's still in the public domain, always will be. He isn't my type." She hesitated, then said in a gentler tone:

"He isn't your type either, darling."

"Why not?"

"Well, he just isn't. In the first place, he's older, more sophisticated, has different ideas about life. What I mean is," Linda said desperately, "he's as wild as any of those Texas broncos he likes to talk about. Wilder, I suspect."

"I could tame him. It would be fun."

Linda flushed, realizing that she herself had harbored the foolish idea of reforming Chris Osborne. But only as an altruistic gesture, a public service; most certainly not for fun.

"You couldn't possibly cope with him, Suzy," she said flatly. "Besides, he isn't good for you."

Resolutely, she closed her lips against further admonitions. This, she decided, was no time to discuss Chris Osborne's shortcomings with a bemused teenager who had mis-identified him as a bona fide Young Lochinvar out of the West. Later, perhaps, but not now.

"How would *you* know he's not good for me? How would *you* know he's not my type? You say you only met him last night, and you met me only a few minutes ago," Suzy pointed out.

Linda, put on the spot, forced a smile and said with conscious inadequacy, "Well, after all, dear, I'm your sister, so why shouldn't I know what's best for you?"

"My stepsister," Suzy corrected without smiling. "And you're talking just like Mother, who always thinks *she* knows best." Adroitly, she eluded the arm Linda tried to put around her.

"All right. I'm only your stepsister. But we're going to be like real sisters and love each other, once we get acquainted. I'm sure of that," Linda vowed — and wished she could believe it.

Suzy's answer was a defiant toss of her blonde head which was far more expressive than words.

Still shaken from the meteoric plane flight, the wild ride into the city, and smarting under the impact of this encounter with a hostile young stepsister, Linda sought refuge in the golden area of silence. Instantly, her thoughts returned to her own sorry plight, this time racing ahead into the misty future.

She had indeed moved too fast too soon. Now here she was, an alien in a strange land, entering a household where, apparently, luxury was taken for granted and family affection was a lost art. Father, her one friend, was away, and she had yet to meet Esther, her stepmother. If Esther was anything like her daughter Suzy —

Linda caught her breath sharply, appalled at the trend of her thoughts. She must not jump to conclusions. Whatever the future held, she must meet it with the patience and kindly understanding that had been an integral part of her training as a nurse. The fact that she was no longer a nurse was inconsequential.

As for Suzy — Father had been right when he had said the child needed an older sister, a down-to-earth companion. Suzy, also, was moving too fast and too soon, really asking for trouble.

Therefore her own duty was clear, Linda concluded. She must forget all about rehabilitating the bucking bronco that was Christopher Osborne. She would have her hands full taming the wild filly that was her young stepsister Suzy.

5

IN the crowded days that followed, care took a holiday. Linda had no occasion for misgivings, no reasonable reason for regrets, little time for soul-searching. Even the urge to purge young Suzy of her false values lost impetus in the exciting activities of the moment, along with the conviction that there was no immediate need for it. The matter of taming the wild filly, Linda decided, could wait for a more propitious time.

Meanwhile Suzy, back in school after what she described to her classmates as 'a colassal weekend,' was also biding her time. Having fired her opening guns on the day of her stepsister's arrival, she appeared to have retired from active combat, accepting Linda's presence as just another cross to be borne by a hapless teen-ager in an adult world.

Oh, there was nothing personal about Suzy's chip-on-the-shoulder attitude. Linda, bending over backward to be scrupulously fair, was convinced of that. It was simply a normal manifestation of the teen-age syndrome; nothing that time, sisterly affection and guidance could not correct. Certainly nothing to get steamed up about.

Suzy, she believed, was running true to form. Smarting under the growing pains peculiar to her age, indulgently misnamed 'youth's divine discontent,' the girl's grudge was against life in general rather than any one individual; resentment against a world she never made, but had the tough luck to live in. The same thing, Linda reflected further, was true of Chris Osborne to some extent. Only surely he was old enough to know better.

I was just as ornery when I was Suzy's age, Linda decided. I carried on something terrible when Father remarried — and he couldn't have picked a finer woman than Esther.

Late in the afternoon on the day of Linda's arrival, Esther had returned from her altruistic mission, admittedly tired but smiling happily over the success of her project. Instantly the villa, whose story-book setting, unsmiling menservants and exotic furnishings had seemed awesome at first, had become home.

Linda had known at once that she was going to like this pretty woman whose steady gray eyes and unaffected manner reflected friendliness of a rare quality. Except for the shining blonde hair they had in common, there was no resemblance whatsoever between mother and daughter.

"We're thrilled to have you with us, darling," Esther said, throwing her arms around her stepdaughter in a spontaneous gesture of affection. "We've wanted you all the time. Now, more than anything, we want you to be happy, know you're loved, have fun."

"It will be fun just living here. I didn't know what I was missing."

"Well," Suzy said, thrusting herself into the scene, "you've been missing a lot of frustrations, hardships and stuff. That's for sure."

Yes, that was true in some respects, Esther agreed. Life as a foreigner in any country was not the perennial picnic it was supposed to be. However, weren't there problems of one kind or another everywhere in the world?

"We even do our own laundry, and there are loads of it," Suzy announced sourly. "Can you imagine anything more degrading? 'Houseboys mustn't tamper with American washing machines; they might break them,'" she quoted her mother in a mimicking tone of voice.

Linda had been unable to suppress a smile. No stranger to hardships, she could see nothing arduous, much less degrading, about doing one's personal washing. Evidently Suzy, in her young discontent, would find fault with living accommodations in the Garden of Eden itself!

"Most of our house servants are tribesmen," Esther explained. "They are not of a mechanical turn of mind. Moreover, they speak in various tribal dialects, so communication is sometimes a problem.

"But I'm a fine one to complain about the servant problem, aren't I?" she added, laughing. "Back home in the States, I was lucky to have a cleaning woman once a week."

Suzy had not finished with her grim picture of life in the tropics. "And you should see the way things fall apart — including people. Not to mention the creepy clothes we're supposed to wear for health reasons. 'Cool, loose garments that will allow freedom of movement and withstand daily washings,'" she'd quoted scornfully. "No wonder everyone looks pregnant. Even men, with their flapping shirt-tails and — "

"That's enough, dear," her mother reproved. "We don't want Linda to get the wrong impression. Now, run along and get into some decent clothes." Helplessly, she'd eyed her daughter's skimpy stretch pants and skintight overblouse and addressed her stepdaughter:

"I don't know what's come over the child. She has lovely clothes. But I no more than leave the house before she's poking around in the poor-box, coming up with some disreputable outfit like the one she's wearing now." Then, to Suzy:

"Run along, dear. Didn't you hear Mother?"

Suzy made a face. "Oh, Mother, how prehistoric can you get? All right," she said sulkily, "I'll go change." But she had not left the room.

Linda, recognizing the 'disreputable outfit' as a teen-age uniform of sorts, felt a stab of compassion for this woman and girl who were so closely akin, and yet were unable to communicate as mother and daughter. There was something to be said for both sides, she'd felt.

Momentarily it had occurred to her that she herself was not in the clear, could easily be classified as prehistoric. Hadn't she disapproved of Chris Osborne's modern hairdo, belittled Suzy's school-girlish crush on the unpredictable young man?

Oh, well, she'd promised herself, I'll make it up to Suzy and to Chris.

"Don't let Suzy discourage you, Linda, my dear," Suzy's mother was saying. "She's in one of her moods. It will pass. She knows very well there are compensations that more than make up for the hardships, as she calls them." Ignoring her daughter's sniff, Esther had proceeded to enumerate what she declared to be only a few of those compensations.

"In the first place, we have air conditioning all over the house, a luxury we've never had before . . . "

"Mother!" Suzy had wailed. "Now you really are being ridiculous. We've never needed it before."

"Furthermore, the people of our host country are not only friendly; they're — "

"Why shouldn't they be friendly, Mother? Just look at the way — "

" . . . progressive, resourceful and deeply religious. We, as a family, also have our personal interests. Robert, your father, has his mining career; I have my charity projects; and Suzy — "

"What have I got?" the girl demanded, pulling a long face.

"You have your school work, dear, and a host of young friends."

"But no boy friends. Only fresh kids I wouldn't wipe my foot on, on account of they still don't know up from down."

"You're only a child yourself, darling," Esther had pointed out, as if that explained everything — which it did, in Linda's opinion.

Suzy, tossing her head in disdain, had come out with the usual fledgling defense: "You don't seem to realize, Mother, that you only live once — and that's when you're young."

Whereupon Linda had made a mental note to have a heart-to-heart talk with her impertinent young stepsister. Esther meant so well, was so right, while Suzy was obsessed with the idea that everybody was out of step but herself.

Dismissing the little byplay with an indulgent smile, Esther had continued: "As for you, Linda, my dear, you'll enjoy the gay social life. Robert and I both feel you've been working too hard, should have a change from your hospital routine, freedom from responsibility. Here, it's a continuous merry-go-round for those who like that sort of thing. Most women here like to entertain, and Americans away from home welcome every chance to get together after business hours."

"But, Mother," Suzy had protested, unable to remain silent any longer, "what will Linda use for men? You know very well there isn't a man in the whole colony that isn't in somebody's doghouse or on the end of a leash. Except, perhaps, that wonderful Mr. Osborne, and she doesn't like the way he combs his hair."

Esther, undaunted, waved a hand in dismissal of the idea. She was well aware of the shortage of eligible men in the colony, she admitted. Most men got married before going on overseas assignments. But there were still a few unattached ones, and others would be arriving at frequent intervals. She anticipated no difficulty finding suitable escorts, if not a real Prince Charming, for a young woman as lovely as Linda.

"You don't need to worry about me," Linda said quickly — too quickly, she realized when Esther laughed softly, knowingly, and said:

"Of course, dear. Your Mr. Right is waiting for you back in the States. Let's hope he doesn't get too impatient and steal you away from us any time soon."

Linda, smiling self-consciously, let it go at that. There was no point in humiliating herself, no reason to bare wounds that were as yet unhealed, might never heal. No one must ever suspect that for the rest of her life she would measure every man she met by the yardstick that added up to Gregory Arnold, M.D. It was most unlikely that she would find so much as a reasonable facsimile.

Two days later, Father had returned from his business trip to Ghana — the same wonderful person Linda had known in the old days. The warmth of his greeting brought tears to her eyes; lit a candle in her heart that surely nothing could extinguish.

Miraculously, her belated cablegram, along with her earlier letter, had been delivered on the very same day, sweeping away any misgivings and leaving no room for errant doubts.

Then, as if some fairy godmother had arranged it, Linda was swept off her feet to become airborne on a dazzling cloud of social activity. Obviously, hospitality was a way of life among the repatriate Americans in the tropical Paradise.

There were parties all over the place — 'the place' being fashionable Mamba Point where only in-people lived. The awareness that most of these galas were being held for the purpose of welcoming her into the charmed circle was all the more bedazzling. Now and then Father would say teasingly:

"So you're getting the red carpet — huh? Well, that's as it should be, honey. But don't let it go to your pretty head. Any day now there'll be other new arrivals, and you'll have to turn over the crown." And Linda would answer, just as lightly:

"Why, of course, Father. I'll admit I'm having loads of fun, really working at it. But I'm not likely to get ideas. I could never in the world change myself." At this point she would lower her eyes, knowing in her heart that she was trying her utmost to do that very thing.

"Well don't wear yourself out, baby. November is flying. Before you realize it, Christmas will be coming up. Then you *will* have to work at having fun. We foreigners make our own Christmas, including the tree."

"You're joking. I've never seen so many gorgeous trees. How could we possibly make one, and why should we?"

"You'll find out. This isn't New England, you know. Tropical trees do not take kindly to indoor captivity."

The remaining days of November — hot and humid, but breathtakingly beautiful in their floral grandeur — flew by on magic wings; Linda, in her ersatz role of butterfly, flying along with them. Each day was a glamorous adventure in a rose-colored stratosphere that appeared to have no tangible beginning, no foreseeable end.

Only the nights — between midnight and daybreak — were left for remembering, for weeping. And surely these poignant moments would grow more infrequent as time and distance laid healing hands on her heart. This Linda firmly believed, *had* to believe.

Aside from this, there was only one small cloud against the horizon: the purely feminine notion that her modest wardrobe would not survive her brief heyday. Suzy had been right when she had said things fell apart in the tropics. And dresses bought with an eye to stylewise economy were not taking too kindly to the frequent washings that were a health-must in that hostile climate. Moreover, a wardrobe assembled in Boston in late October was not altogether suited to forever-June weather.

However, clothes weren't too important in the colony. Everyone knew it took weeks to get orders from the States, so most people made do with whatever they had and thought nothing of it. Therefore she would cross that bridge if or when she came to it.

Mornings, there were 'coffees,' where women with similar interests met to discuss projects and plans to help the needy in their host country. There seemed to be no limit to Esther's interests — and the hospitality of her friends.

These were followed by luncheons, teas, cocktail parties and buffets, leaving little time for the daily siestas which were also a health-must in the tropics. There was no time to malinger, or even to complain about the enervating inoculations and medications required of all Americans as preventives against endemic diseases.

Pretty soft for the nurses around here, Linda found herself thinking. Nothing to do but to give shots and hand out malaria pills. No repercussions. Nobody has time to get sick, to make trouble.

94

There were delightful dinner parties given by foreign service wives versed in the culinary arts of all nations. Here, exotic foods were served in glamorous surroundings; in a style to which Linda, used to hurried meals in a hospital cafeteria, was unaccustomed. Truly, she was seeing life through the rose-colored end of a custommade stethoscope; finding it hectic, but good.

There were evenings of dining and dancing in the roof garden at the Intercontinental, where the food was superb, the service faultless, the prices astronomical. Here, a name band gave out with the latest pop music and the dance floor was, as Chris Osborne had described it, smoother than glass. Overhead, the sky was a star-studded canopy, while the ocean, far below, was a dramatic backdrop for a neon-festooned city.

There were other enchanted evenings at the 'Palawa Hut,' a picturesque pavilion built in the style of an oversized bamboo hut, complete with fictional 'missionary pot' out front. Here, you could eat your fill of 'Liberian Chop,' then let yourself go, dancing with lighthearted abandon to the feverish beat of high-life tribal drums.

The shortage of unmarried men was no problem, friendly togetherness being the rule. These men worked hard and earnestly on high-tension jobs· in the daytime, and wanted only congenial companionship among their fellow Americans during their leisure hours. They knew the therapeutic value of play as well as the dignity of work. There was no fooling around; no pairing off of couples, no slipping out for clandestine detours; as so often happened in the States. The whole thing was as simple and as innocuous as that.

Moreover, Linda knew she could always count on Chris Osborne, looking somewhat out of character in what he called his 'cotton-pickin' hair-do' — lurking somewhere in the background; presumably girl-watching, but actually waiting for a chance to cut in on whatever partner she happened to have.

It was true that Chris was no prize package, romantically speaking. Even young Suzy appeared to have arrived at that conclusion, and Chris had made it quite clear that he wanted no part of what he called 'the nymphet.' However, Chris was obliging, unattached, and — more important — he was *there*!

Altogether, it was a heady experience for Linda. As a working nurse, she'd thought she'd seen everything: life in all its phases, human nature at its best and its worst.

She had seen people in agonizing pain, even dying, rise to great heights of courage. She had seen others, whose ailments were purely psychomatic but whose selfish demands had all but upset the hospital routine. She had come to believe that life was a challenge to be met — and accepted — with whatever courage one possessed. But never before had she met up with life-at-play.

I was wrong, of course. You get what you ask for, she told herself. I should write and remind Gregory Arnold that all work and no play is no good for him. Only I'd never get to first base. He would still tear his heart out, giving his all and trying to do the impossible.

Besides, why should she write Greg

Arnold about anything? He had not bothered to send her so much as a post card. Nor had anyone else at the hospital!

If only I could forget them as easily as they've forgotten me, she mused. Why, it's as though I never worked there at all! And just look at the way I beat my brains out, thinking I was indispensable . . .

Esther, an intuitive person, must have sensed her stepdaughter's distress. "If you don't hear from your young man right away, don't worry, dear," she told Linda. "Mail from the States is slow-slow, as they say over here."

"If only I could get a post card from *somebody*, or even a newspaper — "

"Newspapers are slower. They come by sea mail, always a month or six weeks old on arrival. This is one of the hardships of living so far away. Just try to look at it this way: no news is good news."

Linda tried to look at it that way. But it was no use. As November slipped away on an iridescent cloud and December came in smiling, there were still moments of uncertainty, desolation.

There were still nights when she would

waken after a recurring dream in which Riverview Hospital was going up in flames; patients, their faces ravaged with pain and fear, were crying out for help — and there was neither a doctor nor a nurse in sight.

It was a foolish dream, to be sure, because nowhere in the world was there a hospital safer and more adequately staffed than Boston's Riverview. The loss of one renegade nurse was no tragedy.

Afterwards, for what seemed like hours, she would lie awake, staring out into the black darkness of an African night, wondering, worrying. Vaguely conscious of the hum of the air conditioner in her room, the cloying fragrance of over-ripe flowers, she would find herself plagued by questions:

Why were there no letters from friends and co-workers? Where were the grapevine reports they'd promised to send air mail? What actually was happening at the hospital?

Had the cancer patient in Ward D, who had had so much to live for, given up the piteous struggle? Had the youngster in Ward A with the kidney transplant recovered and gone back to his home and his beloved Little League? What about young Mrs. Canfield, an innocent victim of a crippling prenatal drug? She had wanted her baby so desperately. Had the baby been born? Was it normal?

And was Gregory Arnold, Resident, still working round the clock; still trying to outwit the inevitable? Would he never learn that medicine was not yet an exact science — that no matter how hard you worked, how desperately you prayed, you could not always win?

Were he and Babs still planning to get married in January? Or had Babs changed her mind again and decided to wait for a more favorable time? That time being when Greg would have finished his residency and opened an office of his own . . .

Questions, questions, questions. But Linda could find no answers. For all she knew, Riverview was no longer in existence, all of her favorite patients were long dead — and Gregory Arnold and Babs Green were already married!

6

UNABLE to shut off the playback of memory, Linda became increasingly restless. Plagued by a growing desire to be needed, she could not dismiss the painful conviction that she did not belong anywhere, least of all on the plush playgrounds of an ailing world. The thought that she had charted her own course was but small comfort.

As a kind of self-imposed penance, she joined young Suzy's group on several occasions. Resolutely she tried to take part in the merrymaking at beach parties and at the Intercontinental's swimming pool, feeling every inch a Methuselah among the irrepressible teen-agers.

It did no good to remind herself that she was not yet twenty-two. Evidently in the eyes of these go-go youngsters, she was a back number, the product of another and strictly passé generation. Oh, they were courteous enough, but they contrived to make it clear that she was cramping their style and might better have remained home, knitting.

Only Chris Osborne, whose appearance was always greeted by girlish squeals and envious boyish grins, seemed to have mastered the secret of lasting adolescent approval. No offense was taken at his cavalier behavior, and his outspoken appraisal that they were 'just a bunch of dumb kids with rocks in their heads' never failed to elicit spasms of laughter.

"I don't know how you do it," Linda told him one afternoon when he crashed a gay swimming-pool soiree. "I've been beating my brains out trying to be friends with these kids. All I get is double-talk and dirty looks. Then you barge in, belittling them, saying dreadful things, and right away the boys start lionizing you, and all the little girls are eating out of your hand."

"Could be you're the wrong sex," Chris bantered, with his customary disregard for the amenities — and common decency, Linda felt. "Could be."

"Well," she flared, "I don't like it one bit. You're a bad influence. In fact, it's disgraceful the way you follow these kids around and try to horn in on their fun, you cradle robber!"

Chris looked genuinely hurt. "You've got me dead wrong," he said soberly. "I'm not interested in the fresh little monsters. It's *you* I'm following around. I'm in love with you — or didn't you know?"

"I certainly didn't know — and I couldn't care less!"

"Shucks. You do so know. Why else would I be wearing this cotton-pickin' hair-do?" With that, Chris began laughing again, and Linda had to laugh, too.

"I was right the first time," she told him. "You really *are* impossible, Chris Osborne, and I'm beginning to be afraid it's catching."

Still seeking escape from the turmoil within her, Linda made another overture on behalf of the teen-agers. She offered to organize a Teen-time Club where they could dance and otherwise engage in clean, wholesome fun, only to have young Suzy veto the idea — oh, very politely, of course, but quite firmly.

"We know you mean well, Sis," she said. "But we'd rather do it ourselves."

To Linda, it was some consolation to realize that her stepsister's attitude toward her was changing; that Suzy was beginning to trust if not actually like her. But it wasn't enough. It did nothing to assuage the pain in her heart, or to shorten the long, anxious nights when she was alone with her memories.

Finally, she spoke to Esther about joining the group of women who spent two mornings a week engaged in altruistic pursuits on behalf of the needy. Surely work of this kind would appease the most scrupulous conscience.

"I'm afraid I was never meant to be a playgirl," Linda apologized, aware of the many things that were being done for her pleasure. "Or maybe I waited too late to start."

Esther, always understanding, smiled and said, "Robert and I were hoping you'd be content to relax and enjoy yourself for a while. But if you feel you'd be happier doing something, by all means join us. It's a fine idea."

Suzy, present at the time, tossed her blonde ponytail, indicating how little she thought of the idea. "You'll hate yourself," she told Linda. "They're dull as ditchwater — Mother's hen-parties. Just a lot of old ladies, yak-yaking about what's the world coming to and how come somebody doesn't do something about it. All they do is sew things, and there are never enough scissors and stuff to go around."

"We do what we can with whatever funds we have available," Esther explained. "Right now we're making things for hospitals and schools. It's only simple sewing, drawing and such. As a professional nurse, you won't find the work very challenging. But you'll be doing something useful, and we need all the help we can get . . . "

"It must be fun being a nurse," Suzy chimed in. "I'm thinking about being one myself, some day. I can't imagine anything more fascinating. I always thought I wanted to be a jet hostess, though I may change my mind."

"My dear child," Esther reproved, "you haven't the faintest idea what you're talking about. Nurses have to work hard, very hard. It involves years of training and sacrifice."

"I still say it's fun," Suzy persisted. "After all, they're free to live their own lives. Besides, just look at all the exciting people they meet: famous doctors, cute interns, rich patients and stuff. Marry them, too!"

"Only in romantic novels, darling, and on television," Linda pointed out. "As for freedom — well, a nurse is never really free. She belongs to the profession, the humanities. Once she trains for service, gets the feel of it, her life is never her own."

There, I have said it! Linda thought. The very thing I've been trying to disprove, to deny. Hastily she changed the subject.

"I'll do my best to help out with your sewing project," she told Esther, "though I'll admit I'm no great shakes as a seamstress. I've never had much time for the gentler arts. But surely anyone, given needle and thread, can sew simple seams."

Suzy giggled, and Linda, shocked by the condescension implied in her own words, felt her face burn all the way to the roots of her hair.

"Exactly," Esther said, undisturbed.

For two grueling weeks, on Tuesdays and Thusdays, Linda rose at daybreak to drive with her stepmother through the sizzling heat to a temporary workshop that had been set up in the suburbs. There, with more determination than efficiency, she sewed innumerable seams in an earnest effort to do her bit in a program designed to help hospitals, schools and needy persons, often without benefit of thimble or scissors, and always painfully conscious of her shortcomings.

"You should throw me out bodily," she told Esther one day. "I don't belong here, botching things. Just look at this miserable little number." Linda held out for inspection a child's smock which she was in the process of hemming. "Why, no youngster with any pride would wear it to a first-class dog-fight, much less in a school-room!"

Esther, with characteristic kindliness, placed the blame on the shortage of supplies. Needles and scissors had a habit of rusting in humid climates, she pointed out, and even at home thimbles had a way of getting lost.

"Would you like to change over to art work, dear?" she queried in a carefully casual voice. "There's no shortage of materials there. That generous Mr. Osborne at the Intercontinental — your friend Chris' father — has just donated a bountiful supply . . . "

By mutual agreement, Linda transferred from simple sewing to simple art work. Painstakingly she traced maps, lettered and colored ABC charts to be used in rural schools, feeling for all the world like a square peg in a round hole. Clearly, neither sewing nor drawing was her forte. As much as she hated to admit it, her heart was not in this praiseworthy form of escapism. Finanlly, in desperation, she confessed to her stepmother:

"I don't belong here either. You and your friends are performing a wonderful service. But it takes me forever to do the least little thing, and then it's all wrong."

"You're doing fine, dear," Esther encouraged her. "None of us is an expert. If only you weren't such a perfectionist — "

Linda shook her head. "No such thing.

I'm just tilting at windmills. I might as well face it."

Tilting at windmills. The words rang a bell in the back of her mind. Where had she last heard that quaint expression? Oh, yes, on the plane between Dakar and Monrovia, in a chance encounter with one Paul Raymond, a runaway doctor turned medical missionary.

Medicine — and that included nursing, of course — was a 'sticky' profession, he'd pointed out. Once you had pledged yourself in the cause, you could never get it out of your system. It was, in fact, a heart condition, and incurable.

"I tried to get away from it," he'd said, or words to that effect. "For almost two years I dug ditches, built roads, taught school — tilting at windmills, so to speak. It took me that long to find out I couldn't win." And then he had added a punch line which Linda remembered with sharp accuracy:

"The self you have to live with won't let you fold up and quit."

In any case, Linda concluded, she had an edge on Dr. Paul Raymond in one respect. She had discovered in less than two months what it had taken him almost two years to find out: the fallacy of self-escape. But, unlike him, she had done nothing about it.

Right now, in the sweltering rain forests of Equatorial Africa, Paul Raymond was slaving over a red-hot microscope and ministering to the underprivileged sick, content in the knowledge that he was fulfilling his destiny. Whereas she, a renegade nurse, in air-conditioned comfort, was still tilting at windmills.

True to his word, the crusading doctor had tried to reach Linda by telephone during his brief stop-over in Monrovia. But she had been out partying at the time, and Suzy had taken the message.

"He said there's an emergency back at the clinic where he works, so he was taking the first plane out," Suzy had reported with the importance of one entrusted with a military secret. "He wants you to have this," she added, handing Linda a slip of paper upon which she had written:

Paul Raymond, M.D., Public Health Clinic and Research Center, Bugaboo Village, Free Republic of Marimbia.

"I thought at first he was kidding," Suzy confessed. "After all, 'bugaboo' is what they call ant-hill bricks around here. But he sounded like such a nice man, though I've never heard of a place, even in Africa, name of Marimbia. Sounds like a musical saw or something."

"It's one of the new states, dear," Esther had pointed out. "It's nearer the Equator and considerably hotter than here. The rainy seasons, lasting from April to October, are quite devastating, I've been told."

"Sounds pretty ghastly," Linda had commented, unable to visualize anyone, even a dedicated doctor, having the stamina to work in such a desolate spot. Esther must have sensed her thoughts, for she'd said:

"I'm sure it takes a lot of courage to set up shop there. It's endemic to malaria and other tropical diseases, but the need is great and the opportunities for helpfulness unlimited. Unfortunately, there is still considerable unrest, especially among the tribespeople, I'm told. You know, they're apprehensive of change and resentful of anything that interferes with their traditions. All of which is quite understandable, of course."

"Sounds luscious to me," Suzy had exclaimed, giggling. "Oh boy! Tribal uprisings, talking drums, devil dances, witch doctors and stuff. Maybe cannibals." She sighed. "Nothing really bloodthirsty ever happens around here. Never anything exciting. Only peace, which is anything but wonderful as far as I'm concerned."

Why, you miserable little savage, you're worse than a cannibal, Linda had thought. Aloud she had said to Esther:

"Then you know about the clinic there?"

Esther had nodded. "It's one of the senior Mr. Osborne's pet philanthropies, so we've heard all about it. In fact, in return for his kindness to us women-folk, we've promised to help out as much as we can with routine supplies. Just as soon as we finish our current project, we'll be rolling bandages, collecting bottles, and doing all sorts of things."

At the mention of Chris' 'old man' in the role of dogooder, Linda's jaw dropped, and so did Suzy's, but it was

Suzy who spoke first.

"Mr. Osborne?" she'd jeered. "You mean that old creep who goes around persecuting everybody, including his own son? Why, from where I sit — "

Esther, for the first time since Linda had known her, spoke with acid sharpness. "From where you young upstarts sit, all adults are creeps. You don't realize that we're at our wits' end trying to keep you from destroying yourselves and the world you live in. You have a whole lot to learn, Suzy."

"Suzy's young, Esther. I was just as intolerant when I was her age." Linda, although she shared her step-mother's opinion, had felt impelled to defend the girl. However, in the interest of peace, she'd added with genuine sincerity:

"With you as a mother, I'm sure she has all the makings of a fine woman."

Her reward was twofold. Esther's smile was one of complete reassurance. But Suzy's quick kiss on the cheek was a concession she was to remember, later, as a turning point in the girl's hostile attitude.

Again, she'd made a mental note to

have a sisterly talk with young Suzy. As for Chris Osborne, who should know better than to malign his elders — well, she could hardly wait for a chance to give that incorrigible young man a piece of her mind!

After the sewing-circle fiasco and the equally frustrating sortie into art work, Esther, always sympathetic, came up with a suggestion calculated to solve, once and for all time, the problem of her stepdaughter's unrest. Immediately after the Christmas holidays, she promised, she and Robert would speak to the doctor in charge of the American Health Unit on Linda's behalf.

"That poor dear man," she sighed. "It's up to him to keep all of us well in this climate. He is also responsible for the health of our fellow-Americans in the neighboring states of Mali, Sierra Leone, and heaven knows where else. He must be run ragged. I am sure he would welcome the help of another qualified nurse — like you, my dear," she told Linda.

"Oh, Mother, how unrealistic can you get?" Suzy wailed, unexpectedly coming to her stepsister's rescue. "You know darn well he brings his nurses from the States. Government nurses, who've had to cut miles and miles of red tape; maybe be elected by popular vote, though I wouldn't know about that. Anyhow, they do everything. What, for crying out loud, would Linda do?"

"Shush, dear. He'll find something."

Suzy, having stumbled upon a new cause to champion, did not shush. "Oh, something like washing bottles, answering telephones, putting on band aids, handing out antimalaria pills." She whirled around to face Linda, and her smile conveyed genuine warmth, even sisterly affection.

"You aren't that kind of a nurse, are you, Sis?" There was an unmistakable note of pride in the girl's voice. "From where I sit, you're the real article, not just a filler-in. I can't see you settling for anything less than something super-special."

Linda returned the girl's smile and declined, with a proper show of appreciation, Esther's well-meaning offer. If or when she returned to nursing, it would not be to perform such

115

inconsequential tasks as washing bottles, answering telephones and applying band aids.

It remained for Suzy to set off the bombshell that was to turn the tide of indecision into action. One Saturday afternoon when Linda and Esther returned from a luncheon held for the purpose of discussing ways and means of helping the clinic in Marimbia, they found Suzy standing at the front door, her blue eyes alight with excitement. Her expression, Linda observed, was not unlike that of a sly kitten who has raided a cream jar and found the contents gooey but good.

"He was *here*!" Suzy announced breathlessly. "Right here in this house! And he's marvelous! I've never seen such heartbreaking eyes. I could bawl right now, just remembering them."

"Who was here?" Suzy's mother demanded.

"Who's so marvelous you feel you want to cry?" Linda queried.

"Why, your Dr. Paul Raymond, of course," Suzy said without hesitation. "I tried to keep him till you got here, even offered him tonic and cookies, which is all I'm allowed to serve — "

"Never mind that, dear." Esther broke in. "You're still only a child. But what happened?"

"He went. There was a car waiting outside to take him back to the airport. He was only stopping off between planes, was already due back at the clinic, he said. I'm sorry," she told Linda. "I tried my best to keep him." She turned to Esther.

"You don't need to worry any more about Sis, Mother. She's joining the Army. I only wish it was me."

"What do you mean, I'm joining the Army?" Linda gasped.

"We-e-ll," Suzy hedged, "that nice Dr. Raymond of yours called it a war, a war on tropical diseases and stuff. He said it would be only a matter of time till you were in there, fighting. How about it, Sis?"

Linda, annoyed at what she considered unwarranted interference in her personal affairs, counted to ten before she spoke. "What else did he have to say for himself — and for me?" She was convinced that

Suzy, who had all the tenacity of the cat Curiosity killed, had made the most of her chat with the officious doctor.

Suzy thought a minute, evidently separating what she knew from what she wanted to tell. "For one thing, he said you won't be able to live with yourself till you get back into the groove where you belong. And I told him he was so right, considering how hard you were working to live and have fun with other people . . . "

"Suzy!" Esther warned, raising her voice to an unEstherlike pitch. "What on earth are you chattering about? I'm sure I don't know, and I don't think you do either."

"Linda knows, don't you, Sis?" Suzy giggled, as though she had chanced upon a secret worthy of further exploration.

"Maybe I do know, but — but — " Linda stammered, her face reddening. "Only you seem to know a lot more about this thing than I do."

"Could be," Suzy agreed airily. "At least I know he's counting on hearing from you, and soon; expecting you to join him in that exciting hot spot."

"Well, now, isn't that fine? I suppose I have nothing to say about it!"

"Oh, but you have so," Suzy protested, changing her tactics. "He didn't sound the least bit bossy; just hopeful. Said the decision was entirely up to you. Said there was no point trying to convince a woman against her will. He even stammered a couple of times — the poor man."

"That was his corny Southern accent, honey," Linda blurted, torn between resentment and compassion. "But don't get me wrong. I'm sure Dr. Paul Raymond is a fine person — dedicated and all that sort of thing. But he would do well to mind his own business. What else did you needle him into saying?"

"I didn't have to needle him." Suzy looked aggrieved, and buttoned her lips momentarily. "He said a lot. But the main thing was that you were to make up your mind all by yourself, then write him a letter telling him when you'll be there."

"It seems," Linda said pointedly, "that you and the conniving Paul Raymond have already made up my mind. So all

119

I have to do is write the letter. What is this — a conspiracy?"

Nevertheless, she smiled as she spoke.

Later, in the privacy of her room, Linda wrote briefly to Dr. Paul Raymond, offering her services in whatever capacity she might be useful, through the emergency that would last only through the rainy season, she assumed. She would spend Christmas with the family, of course, she pointed out, but would be available immediately thereafter. Dutifully she attached a résumé of the work she had done, a list of her credentials.

As she sealed and stamped the envelope for tomorrow's mailing, she was conscious of a vast sense of release; as though a heavy weight had been lifted from her conscience. Very soon, with any luck and only a reasonable amount of red tape, she would be back in the groove where her heart was, always would be: nursing.

7

CHRISTMAS WEEK came in smiling, with no visible change in circumstances, except that the social pomp was stepped up to what Linda thought was the point of saturation. Homesick Americans were going all out to prove to themselves and one another that home was where the parties were, and that togetherness was the one infallible cure for nostalgia.

Meanwhile, the sky was just as cloudless, the flowers as fragrant, the heat as static, as they were supposed to be during the six-months dry season. The villas were a kaleidoscope of brilliant color: twinkling lights and gay wreaths proclaimed the news that the season of peace and good will was at hand. The various Gardens of Eden were blooming and ready. So were the people.

To Linda, accustomed to the snowy whiteness of New England winters and the modest *divertissements* available to hard-working nurses, it was a unique experience: this combination of heat and humidity, fragrance and festivity, and of frenzied activity in the interest of fun. She said as much one evening when the Harlan family had gathered together in the living room to work on the tree, which Father had warned would be 'made from scratch.'

"Christmas is Christmas, wherever you are, girls," Father observed. As he spoke, he placed a king-size floor lamp on top of a large wooden box that Esther had already shrouded in green crepe paper.

Esther, who was now fashioning wire coat hangers into limbs for the ersatz tree, paused to blow her husband a kiss. "You're so right, darling."

Suzy, in the process of stringing popcorn for festoons, groaned aloud. It was clear that this do-it-yourself performance did not appeal to her; she was simply going along with it because she could think of no practicable means of escape.

"Seems sort of silly to me," she commented. "There are scads of beautiful Christmas trees down at the market, shipped in all the way from Denmark. Surely we can afford one."

"I agree with you, Suzy," Father applauded as he began, with no great success, to fill the various open spaces with green tissue paper. "I've a good notion to tear this monstrosity apart with my bare hands. Certainly we can afford a real tree."

"Don't get excited, my dears," Esther reproved gently, addressing the two rebels. "Christmas, like life, is what one makes of it. It's the spirit that counts: the love you weave into your gifts, the satisfaction of doing things with your hands."

She's right, of course, as always, Linda reflected, and felt a curious stab of resentment. Her sympathy this time was all with Father and with Suzy. It was not easy to cope with perfection. Looking back, she could recall plenty of times when she herself had been irritated by Gregory Arnold's unfailing rightness, though she'd accepted her own inevitable wrongness as the cause of it all.

In any case, there was no gainsaying the fact that Esther was making a production of her rightness, happily unconscious of the fact that her velvet gloves were slipping and her iron hands starting to show. Linda was secretly pleased to see Father take a vicious swipe at the current bone of contention, all but toppling the skeleton tree from its moorings, and to hear Suzy say:

"Don't mind what Mother says, Robert. She always goes corny around Christmas time. Even if we work our fingers to the bone, this dreadful thing" — she indicated the tree — "will never be anything but a monstrosity, like you said. We could be right, both of us, for a change."

They were wrong. Once the tree was finished and the decorations added, it was beautiful. The makeshift background was completely obscured by twinkling lights in myriad colors and quaint Christmas ornaments that Father and Esther had collected in their travels. These were augmented by gayly colored bells and make-believe icicles bought in downtown Monrovia.

Suzy's popcorn festoons and Linda's miniature gilded gourds, along with a star-studded angel which Esther had made from what she described as 'whole cloth,' completed the festive display.

Father, manlike, was all for taking the credit himself, straight through from the inception of the idea to its execution. But the laughter that greeted his remarks gave him pause.

"All right, girls; you win." He chuckled. "What chance has a mere man got when three beautiful dolls are running the show? We did this remarkable job together, as a family, and in the true Christmas spirit. Shall we give our masterpiece a name?"

"Sure thing." Suzy giggled. "How about calling it a mystery tree and playing games at our Open House on Christmas Eve? Nobody — and I do mean *nobody* — will ever guess what it's made of."

"I've got a better idea," Esther said. "We'll call it 'the tree that Love built.' How's that for corn? Now go ahead and laugh, everybody," she challenged.

Nobody laughed. Surprisingly, Suzy flung her arms around her mother and kissed her gently on the cheek. "Nothing corny about that, Mom," she caroled. "I think you've got something there. You were right about another thing, too. It really is fun doing things with our hands."

"Thank you, darling." There were tears in Esther's eyes as she spoke, prompting Linda to say with no regard whatsoever for corn:

"Something tells me this is going to be a special Christmas — super-special, in fact."

From Linda's point of view, the week preceding Christmas was special in many respects. First of all, 'the boat' came in, bringing great bales of newspapers from home. True, they were weeks old and there were pre-Christmas parties to attend. Nevertheless, she sat up nights, almost until daybreak, trying to catch up on the news. She scanned every line of the Boston dailies, thinking to find at least one small item that would give her an inkling of some of the things she wanted so very much to know.

There were stories about political hassles, urban renewal, racial imbalance, demonstrations, public housing, bank robberies, crime and punishment. There were weather warnings, social notes, household hints, fashion fantasies, obituaries. But none of these included the names of anyone Linda knew.

There was almost nothing about Riverview Hospital. Only two small items, one of which pointed out a fact she already knew: Riverview, always a model of efficiency, was adjusting most effectively to the growing demands of Medicare and other humanitarian projects. The other item mentioned briefly a new wing that was to be added soon for the purpose of medical research. That was all.

As a last resort, she pored over the advertisements, even the want ads, on the absurd premise that some item might have escaped her. But somehow she could not get excited over the ex-news that Filene's 'Thanksgiving Giveaway' would undoubtedly top all previous sales, and that Jordan Marsh was arranging a pre-Christmas sale that would surely go down in mercantile history.

However, to offset her disappointment in the news media of her beloved New

England, there was a perfect deluge of Christmas cards, many of which included personal notes. These, too, were disappointing, in a way. While they were full of fond greetings and wish-you-were-here messages, they contained nothing in the way of news that Linda could sink her teeth into. Either the grapevine had gone out of business, or the assumption was that their former co-worker knew all she needed to know about what actually went on in the more intimate environs of the hospital.

"You'd think they'd put up a wall just to exclude me," Linda murmured aloud, though she could not bring herself to believe any such thing.

There was one letter — from Gregory Arnold! It was a rather long letter, considering how busy and infuriatingly close-mouthed Greg was. Scribbling on both sides of a sheet of paper, he had written at length, mainly about the new research department that was being set up at Riverview. It was, he explained, for the purpose of obtaining the know-how on various tropical diseases.

Why is Riverview getting excited over

tropical diseases? Linda fumed. America isn't the tropics. That's Dr. Paul Raymond's department. Aren't there problems enough without borrowing more? Reading on, she found the answer to at least one of her questions. Greg had written:

'Quite a few service men returning from the tropics are being plagued by malaria and other insidious ailments. More will be coming all the time. The thing to do is to jump the gun. From here on, I'll be neck-deep in research.'

The letter was signed: 'As always, your friend and team-mate, Gregory Arnold, M.D.' The nearest thing to a personal note was a postscript, reading:

'When are you coming back, pal? I hate to say this, but I'm having a rather blunderful time with your featherbrained replacement.'

There was not a word about Babs Green; not so much as a line about their forthcoming marriage and Greg's plans for opening his own office. What had happened? Linda wondered. Why didn't somebody — *anybody* — tell her some of the things she really wanted to know?

8

IT was on Christmas Day in the afternoon when it happened: the incident that turned an otherwise happy holiday into a mockery and fleeting dreams into a nightmare.

Linda, her father and Esther were sitting in the living room, 'taking it easy and holding post-mortems,' as Father laughingly insisted they should do. They were talking over the previous night's open house, which had been an outstanding success, and reiterating their appreciation of gifts received in that morning's family exchange.

For the first time in a week, the villa was quiet and the three were alone. Because today was Christmas to the Liberians, too, and there was still a surfeit of food from last night's party, the servants were taking the afternoon off. And Suzy, as a special holiday treat, had been permitted to go with Christopher Osborne on the long-promised drive to the airport and back.

"Jeepers," Father exclaimed presently. "This place is as still as a morgue without young Suzy around raising the roof. Funny thing about kids. They give you no peace when they're underfoot. But the minute they leave the house it goes dead. You can neither get along with nor without them. Isn't it about time that young squirt was bringing her back?"

"No, love," Esther said. "Don't forget it's fifty miles to the airport, and Chris promised to drive slowly, carefully. They both know they must be back before dark. We're having an early supper-a-pick-up meal — and Chris is joining us."

"He'd *better* get her back before dark," Father grunted. "That is, if he doesn't want me tearing him apart."

"Now, Robert, be fair," Esther reproved. "Come to think of it, Chris didn't seem too enthusiastic about the little outing. Perhaps," she added thoughtfully, "I shouldn't have given Suzy permission, but then — "

"I know," Father said. "It's Christmas,

and our little Suzy knows how to make with the sweet-talk."

Again commenting on the unwonted silence and mumbling something to the effect that families should stay together on Christmas Day, Father went over and turned on the radio full force. A news bulletin was coming over the air, but the reception was poor and not all of the details were clear. However, they were clear enough to strike terror into the hearts of the three listeners. The announcer was saying:

" . . . the girl, apparently still in her teens, has long flaxen hair and is wearing a green shift with white ruffles . . . The man, probably in his mid-twenties, is tall, well-built, and has a blond crew cut. Although no identification has been made up to this time, it is assumed that both are Americans.

"They were picked up by passing motorists, Liberian, and taken to the emergency clinic of a nearby rubber plantation, where the girl's condition is reported as fair and the man has been placed on the danger list. The car, a red racer of European make, was demolished."

No one spoke. There was no need for words. Despite the faulty reception, it was agonizingly clear to the three Harlans that there had been a serious accident, and that the victims were Suzy and Chris. Still without speaking, the stricken trio hurried out of the villa and slid into the family car.

"That would be the Firestone Clinic, near the airport. Fasten your seat belts," Father said. He turned on the ignition, pressed hard on the accelerator, and moments later the vehicle was moving at top speed along the highway.

Involuntarily, Linda shuddered. Once more, as on the day of her arrival in Liberia, she was 'burning the wind' on an open road, with fear in her heart and a silent prayer on her lips. But this time neither the fear nor the prayer was for herself. The prayer was for Suzy, the fear for Chris.

When they reached the small but surprisingly modern clinic, the Harlans were met with good news — and bad. Suzy, aside from shock and surface bruises, was, by some miracle, unhurt. In a few days, the doctor assured them the resilient teen-ager would be as good as new.

"They have remarkable recuperative powers — these youngsters," he pointed out. "Too, this little girl was lucky."

But Chris' was another story, and not at all hopeful. As yet, the full extent of his injuries had not been determined. It was believed, however, that his back was broken. His legs were immobile and, despite sedation, he was still in considerable pain.

"Poor Chris," Linda murmured. "He may never walk again; never smile." Oddly, it seemed to her that the latter was the greater of the two misfortunes. It was true that his mocking grin had irritated her enormously at times. And yet — an unsmiling Chris? Oh, no!

When they left the hospital some three hours later, Linda carried in her mind two living pictures that she was not soon to forget. In fact, they were to remain with her until time and circumstances softened their outlines to blend in with the overall panorama of life.

First, there was the picture of Suzy, her elfin face contorted with grief, lying motionless and desolate on her narrow hospital bed; of Suzy sitting up abruptly, to throw her arms around her stepsister and to cry out:

"I want to die, Sis! I don't want to live another single minute!"

"Shush, honey." Linda held the girl close, stroking the disheveled flaxen hair. "You don't realize what you're saying."

"I do so realize what I'm saying," Suzy sobbed. "And I *do* want to die, right now! Only I can't. You'd want to die, too, if you were in my place. You see — "

"The child's delirious," Esther wailed, and ran to fetch a doctor.

"I am not delirious. Mother doesn't understand. She's never realistic. Even if I told her — " With that, Suzy burst into an uncontrollable fit of weeping.

"Suzy! Stop that kind of talk!" Linda, faced with what she believed to be mounting hysteria, tried to be firm, as a nurse was supposed to be. But it was no use. Somehow she could not bring herself to continue in that vein. Better to reason with the girl, she decided, though Suzy was not given to reasoning when an adult called the turns.

"You don't understand either," Suzy accused her. "Maybe if you'd listen — "

"I do understand, honey," Linda said very gently. "You're upset, as naturally you would be after an accident. But the doctor says you're in good shape, have nothing to worry about, and I'm sure he's right." Purposely, she refrained from mentioning Chris' tragic plight.

"How does *that* old fussbudget know I've got nothing to worry about? How do *you* know?" Suzy pulled away from her stepsister and buried her face in the pillow. "How does anybody know, when they don't even know what I'm talking about and won't let me explain?" she moaned.

"There's nothing to explain, darling," Linda soothed her. "Now try to calm down and get some rest. The doctor will give you a sedative, of course. Don't forget you've had quite a shock."

Suzy turned over to face Linda, her

blue eyes registering a curious mixture of despair and defiance. "There is so something to explain. What I'm trying to tell you is — well, it was all my fault, that dreadful accident. Now maybe I've killed Chris — and I did wreck his beautiful car."

Linda, failing to see the connection, tried to speak lightly. "Oh, come now, Suzy; let's be sensible. You had nothing to do with it. Besides, Chris is still very much alive. And the car doesn't matter one little bit."

"He might as well be dead. His back is broken, and never as long as he lives will he be able to walk again," Suzy stammered between sobs.

"Suzy! You — you don't know that." Linda, taken aback, was stammering too. "Nobody knows for sure, even the doctors . . . "

Suzy shook her head and burst into another spasm of weeping. "The nurses know. I heard them talking. They thought I was unconscious, I guess. Anyhow, it was all my fault, and I'll never be able to live with myself — *never!*"

Esther, who had slipped back into the

room, ran forward, wringing her hands. "You see. I was right. The child *is* delirious. How can she possibly blame herself? It was Chris' car; he was driving. I cautioned him to drive carefully, but you know how young people are."

Suzy sat up very straight and spoke in a harsh little voice that was even more distressing than her tears. "No, Mother, I was driving. At least I was trying to. It was only a few seconds, and Chris was fighting mad."

"*You* were driving?" Esther gasped. "Why, my dear child, you don't know the first thing about cars!"

"Yes, Mother, I was driving — trying to, that is." Suzy glanced at Linda for moral support. "Once Chris promised he'd let me have a turn at the wheel. Remember, Sis? It was the day you came, and he brought you from the airport."

"He didn't really promise, honey," Linda reminded her. "He only said maybe."

"Well, to me it was a promise," Suzy persisted. "Anyhow, I kept needling him. Finally I just grabbed the wheel away from him, fought him right back. And now," she finished on a shuddering sob, "he hates me, and I'll hate myself to the last day I live."

Garbled though the explanation was, it was heartbreakingly clear that Suzy had learned a lesson. But Linda could not dismiss the feeling that the cost was too great.

Then there was the unforgettable picture of Chris, though the tall, athletic figure, which seemed to dwarf the small bed upon which it was lying, bore but faint resemblance to the laughing young man Linda had known. Only the absurd 'cotton-pickin" crew cut looked familiar.

Chris was lying with his eyes closed, his arms flung over his head in a touchingly childlike gesture. He was groaning softly, oblivious to everything except nagging pain which, so far, had refused to respond to medication.

A flustered nurse was hovering over him, doing whatever she could for her patient's comfort, while Christopher Osborne, Senior, stood nearby, watching her every movement with sharply critical eyes.

The old gentleman's expression, Linda

observed, was a changing composite made up of disbelief, outrage, disapproval, and anxiety. Abruptly, he focused his attention upon the colored nurse.

"Do something, young lady!" he commanded. "Don't just stand there. If you need equipment you haven't got around here, I'll buy it." The implication was that he would buy the hospital, if necessary. "No expense is to be spared. Understand?"

"We're doing all we can, Mr. Osborne. And we have all the equipment we need," the nurse said stiffly. "We are well prepared to handle any emergency, as well as any routine case."

"This is *not* a routine case," the old gentleman pointed out. "This is *my* son, my only son. His back is broken, his life over — and he's young, terribly young." There was no bluster in his voice now, and his eyes, so like Chris' were eloquent with naked grief.

The nurse glanced at Linda in mute appeal.

"I'm sure she's right, Mr. Osborne," Linda said earnestly. "They're doing all they can for Chris. And I've never seen a small hospital so well equipped."

He looked at Linda sharply, as though seeing her for the first time. "How would *you* know?" he demanded. "Who are you, anyhow, and why are you here? I was told my son would have complete privacy."

"I know it's a well-equipped hospital," Linda said evenly, "because I am a nurse. I trained and was on the staff of one of the finest hospitals in the States. And I am here because I am Chris' friend."

The old gentleman's manner changed abruptly, and he came forward, both hands outstretched. "Oh. Then you're Linda, the girl he's always talking about." He became officious again, saying with a calm highhandedness that marked him indelibly as his son's father: "You are also the nurse who will attend Chris from now on. I'm taking him away from here. I'm sure my boy will be happier in our own suite at the Intercontinental. Later, if necessary, I shall take him to Europe, for consultation with the finest specialists in the world."

"But I have other commitments," Linda protested. "That is, I've offered my services in the war against tropical diseases in Central Africa."

He waved that information aside with a grandiose gesture. Linda could withdraw her offer, he boomed. In return, he would make a generous donation to the worthy cause. Obviously, like his son, he was of the honest opinion that earth had no problem that cash could not solve.

Wavering between indignation at the old gentleman's officiousness and pity for his unfortunate son, Linda could only stare at him in speechless dismay.

There was a slight movement on the bed, followed by a piteous moan, and Chris opened his eyes; eyes from which all the luster, all the laughter had gone. Seeing Linda, however, his face brightened a little and, with an effort, he reached out a hand to touch her.

"Is it *you* — or am I on one of those LSD trips?" he mumbled.

Linda bent over and brushed her lips against his pallid cheek. "Yes, Chris. It's me — Linda. I came as soon as I could."

"She's staying, too, as long as you're bedridden," Chris' father announced in a falsely jovial voice. "As a matter of fact, she's your nurse from now on. Make you feel better, son?"

Helplessly Linda let it pass, realising she was no match for Chris, let alone Chris' 'old man.'

Then a miracle happened. Chris' taut lips parted in a smile. It was only a ghostly version of its former self, but a smile nevertheless.

"Don't look so glum, Miss Universe," he said with sudden spirit. "It won't be for long. I don't aim to stay bedridden. I'll soon be back on the ball, living it up." Grimacing with pain, he sank back on the pillows in voiceless exhaustion.

Linda turned her face away. Chris, who still did not suspect the extent of his injuries, must not see her cry.

9

THE emotion-packed weeks that followed constituted a major challenge, not only to Linda's skill as a nurse but also her resourcefulness as a woman, while enhancing her stature as a human being. As a reluctant draftee in the Osbornes' luxury suite at the Intercontinental, she soon found herself filling the multiple role of nurse and cheerleader to a helpless young man, intermediary for a stricken father, and sometime balance-wheel for others whose lives had been clouded by the tragic accident.

Chris, no longer in ignorance of the extent of his injuries, was a difficult patient. Although the pain was soon under control and he was the unproud possessor of a handsome wheel chair, there was no promise of ultimate recovery. His morale was suffering accordingly, and his mercurial temperament was no help.

Fundamentally a creature of changing moods and spoiled by an indulgent, though erratic, parent, he was desolate, demanding, arrogant and overly optimistic, by turns. Often he was bitterly resentful of the loving compassion his helplessness inspired.

Most discouraging of all to Linda, accustomed to the tacit rules of self-discipline observed by most hospital patients, was Chris' arrant disregard for such 'trifles' as made nurse-patient relationships compatible. He had a way of leaping abruptly from the lowest depths of despondency to impossible heights of optimism, bypassing less dramatic plateaus in between, and taking his nurse right along with him!

He knows me too well, considers me family, Linda reflected. I suppose there is something to be said for doctors who pass the buck when members of their own family get sick. They know they can't win.

In any case, she reflected further, it was not easy to cope with a male patient who in one breath was deploring the fact that he had ever been born, and the next instant was making plans for living life up in a really colossal way. It was all the more distressing to realize that Chris, unable to face up to his calamity, insisted upon including her in these fanciful plans.

"As soon as I'm back on my own two feet, I'll hock this solid gold gocart," he would say, indicating the hated wheel chair. "Then we'll get married, huh? We'll do Europe on our honeymoon. After that, we'll fly over to God's Country and give little ol' Texas a look-see at another home-town lad who's made good. Okay, Nurse Beautiful?"

And Linda, aware of the therapeutic value of optimism, whatever its form, would cross her fingers and murmur, "Why not?"

Chris, she realized, was whistling in the dark. Surely he knew as well as she did that, barring a miracle, the wheel chair was there to stay. But she must do nothing, say nothing, that might discourage any small evidence of hope on Chris' part. She could only weep in her heart at the pity of it all.

Moreover, if Chris chose to misinterpret

his need for her as a nurse as love for her as a woman, she could do nothing about that either. Not now. Not while he sat in a wheel chair, helpless, unable to move. Under no circumstances, however, must she allow herself to mistake pity, the inner satisfaction of being needed and useful, for a deeper emotion. Nurses were strictly for healing, not feeling.

Distressing, too, was the change that took place in Christopher Osborne, the elder, when neither time nor therapy effected any visible change in his son's physical condition. Gone was his bluster, and there was a defeated look in his eyes which said more plainly than words that, in his considered opinion, life and the Almighty Dollar were letting him down.

"Chris is all I have," he told Linda, as he had so many times before. "From the day he was born, I've tried to give him everything he wanted, though we've never seen eye to eye as to what he should have. Now he has nothing. And I have nothing, less than nothing."

"Oh, but you have, too," Linda protested. "At least Chris is alive, still hopeful. And doctors are performing miracles every day. Besides, you do have money — which a lot of people don't have — and can get the best medical talent available."

The old gentleman shook his head unhappily, as much as to say that all doctors were charlatans, and that money was the greatest fraud of all. It was on the tip of Linda's tongue to point out that Chris' courage, although based on nothing more tangible than wishful thinking, was greater than that of his father.

Not a week passed that did not bring its quota of skilled medical men. They came singly, in pairs, sometimes in small groups; by way of commercial jet, ship or charter plane, from America as well as the various European capitals. The best local doctors were brought in for consultation.

Included in the august assemblage were neurosurgeons, therapists, bone specialists, general practitioners, all tops in their respective fields. In the aggregate, they constituted what Linda felt was a fine nucleus for an International Medical Association, in which only the elect could participate and through which only the chosen few could benefit. She was glad that Chris, by virtue of his father's wealth, was among the latter.

As might have been expected, there was considerable difference of opinion among the great and the neargreat. But the overall consensus was that nothing short of a scientific miracle would effect a permanent cure for the young man who sat immobile in a wheel chair, alternately bemoaning his fate and weaving improbable dreams out of rapidly diminishing hope.

Meanwhile Suzy, still tortured by guilt, began to present a complication. Promptly at four o'clock on week days, en route home from school, she would arrive at the Intercontinental, yearning to make amends to Chris, and inquiring of her stepsister what to do with her life.

"That is, what little there is left of it," Suzy would qualify, smiling bravely. "Now what can I do for poor Chris?"

Whereupon 'poor Chris,' although cringing at the appellation, would join Suzy in the playing of word games which she had brought along for his amusement.

For a half-hour or so they would play earnestly while Suzy alternately expressed her concern for poor Chris and her abhorrence for herself for having caused the fateful accident, apologizing over and over again for the ignominious part she had played. Finally Chris would say, either out of common gallantry or in the interest of peace:

"Couldn't we just skip the post-mortems, Sis? I was to blame for the whole thing. You had nothing to do with it."

"I was so to blame. But you *would* be a gentleman . . . "

"Okay. I'm a gentleman. Mind telling your finefeathered sister and taking a load off her mind? But *must* we play games? Couldn't we do something else, huh?"

"Oh, yes, but of course. I could take you for a ride through the garden, out where the action is."

With a gentle solicitude that would have done credit to her kindly mother, Suzy would wheel Chris through the fragrant gardens that were part of the splendor of the celebrated hostelry; then back and forth along the broad terrace overlooking the swimming pool, where the young in-set gathered in the late afternoons to relax and have fun.

Watching them from a balcony, Linda did not know whether to smile or to frown. She knew very well that Suzy hated word games, calling them fuzzy. And surely Chris could not want anything less than to see and be seen by his more fortunate contemporaries at play. Chris in the role of spectator, with Suzy a dedicated martyr, made an incongruous picture that had to be seen to be believed.

And yet when Linda offered to have a forthright talk with the girl, Chris surprised her by shaking his head and saying:

"Oh, let the kid do her soap opera bit. I'll admit she gets in my hair. But I'd sooner lose an arm than hurt our little ol' Sis. Poor kid, she's had it. Could be she's hurt deeper inside than I am."

Linda smiled encouragement. This was quite a switch, she thought, for a young man who heretofore had assumed he had a monopoly on everything, including the world's most exquisite pain. Certainly she had never regarded compassion as one of Chris' Osborne's outstanding traits. However, Chris was improving — characterwise if not otherwise.

Suzy, too, was improving; she was growing up. As time passed, she talked less and less about 'burying' herself in a nunnery, or becoming a missionary in some far-off, undesignated place. Her plans for the future were taking tangible form, and the question of what to do with her life was gradually being resolved.

She would finish high school, she confided. Then, with her mother's permission and her stepsister's blessings, she hoped, she would go into training for the humanitarian career of nurse.

"I've simply got to do something constructive," she announced gravely. "You know, like helping people. If I don't, I'll die dead. You know what, Sis? There's a whole lot more to life than just having fun," Suzy added with the aplomb of one who has invented a new rule for confident living.

"You have my blessings, honey. You'll make a fine nurse," Linda said, and almost believed it.

"Oh, will I *really*?" Suzy breathed, then answered her own question. "But of course I'll make a fine nurse. I'm your sister, aren't I? And, believe it or not, I'm no slouch as a copycat, once I set my mind to it."

Linda believed that. Time and again the ubiquitous teen-ager had demonstrated the fact that she was no slouch in any department, once she set her mind to it.

Now and then Esther would drop in, resolutely scattering sunshine among all and sundry, but not quite concealing the shadows that lurked behind her wistful smile.

"The child is tearing her heart out, blaming herself for what's happening to Chris," she would tell Linda privately. "I try to help her, but I can't seem to get through to her."

"Try not to worry, Esther," Linda would console. "Let's leave the communications bit up to Suzy. She'll take care of it in her own good time and her own special way. Suzy is growing up."

Often Esther would bring letters from home to Linda. Since Christmas, friends and co-workers back at the hospital appeared to have overcome their collective allergy to correspondence. The grapevine, too, was back in operation. Linda could not count the times she'd been informed that the engagement between Barbara Green, 'birdbrain,' and Dr. Greogry Arnold, 'living doll,' had been canceled.

While there were many fanciful guesses as to what exactly had caused the split-up, it was unanimously agreed that Greg was a lucky man and a changed one. One co-worker, more loquacious than the others, had written:

' . . . And don't think he doesn't know how lucky he is. He goes around grinning from here to there, pretending it's because he's to be in charge of our new research operation. He doesn't realize that the medico who can fool a staff nurse is yet to be born. Now I ask you, isn't that just like a man.'

★ ★ ★

Almost every week there would be a letter from Greg. The first one, undoubtedly written at considerable cost to his pride, had told briefly of the collapse of his marriage plans. Gallantly, he had absolved Babs of any possible blame, declaring that she had good reason to ask for release. He was by no means a matrimonial prize, Greg admitted. His professional duties, along with his research studies, left no time whatsoever for the give-and-take so essential to happy married life.

Linda had answered that letter immediately, expressing her regret over the collapse of his romance and pointing out that he had no reason to belittle himself. And, with incautious loyalty, she predicted that Babs would live to regret having jilted so brilliant a doctor, so wonderful a man.

That was a mistake. Subsequent letters from Greg showed less and less restraint and no humility whatsoever. More and more they took on a romantic flavor and were clearly meant to be a slow-motion prelude to a marriage proposal.

With mixed emotions, Linda would read Greg's letters. Then, with the best of intentions, she would place them in a box reserved for keepsakes, unfinished business and other such appurtenances. Sufficient unto each day were the problems thereof, she reasoned, so the letters would have to wait. She had promises to keep and pledges to fulfill.

As a nurse, she had promised to remain with Chris as long as he needed her. As a human being, she had resolved to stand by Suzy and Esther, while the girl adjusted to life and the two adjusted to each other. As a volunteer, she had pledged herself to serve in the far-off rain forests where people were dying for want of medical personnel.

Altogether, it was a heavy assignment in which Linda could only compromise by doing first things first and getting what satisfaction she could out of the thought that she was fulfilling her destiny. It was distressingly true that Chris' physical condition was not improving, and quite understandably his moods were reacting accordingly. It was equally true that both Suzy and Esther still had their 'moments.' But something would have to give — eventually.

Thus the days passed: an assembly

line of marching hours in which hope and despair, trial and error, smiles and tears, followed one another in relentless succession. The days lengthened into weeks, the weeks into months. And so it was April and the rainy season had started before Linda was free to proceed with other plans.

Her release came unexpectedly. Christopher Osborne, Senior, still sifting the medical world for a cure for his son, learned of a Swiss specialist who was making history in the successful treatment of spinal injuries sustained on the Alpine ski slopes. Miracles were coming to pass, the old gentleman pointed out. What had happened to others would happen to Chris!

His enthusiasm was contagious, and Linda, watching Chris as his father talked and made plans, was heartened to see her patient's expression change from skepticism to interest, from hope to belief. That, too, was catching and soon she found herself believing right along with father, and son. Under the circumstances, only a confirmed Doubting Thomas could have disbelieved.

With his usual flair for getting things done in a hurry, the old gentleman went into action. Phone calls were made, far and near, cablegrams exchanged. Once the specialist's status was confirmed, his record of performance verified, a plane was chartered to be held in readiness for a quick take-off.

In what seemed like no time at all, Chris, with confidence in his eyes and gay promises of a early return on his lips, was on his way to Switzerland and the miracle man. And Linda, feeling strangely bereft, was free to fulfill a pledge made in December and still on the agenda.

"I'll come back walking on my own two feet," Chris promised her when they were saying goodbye at the airport. "Matter of fact, I'll come running like crazy back to my favorite nurse, who also happens to be my true love. You'll wait for me, huh?"

Linda tried to match his gayety. "Pooh, you won't need a nurse. You'll come back rearin' to go and start walking all over everybody in sight — 'riding herd,' as you call it. Oh, I know you, Chris Osborne."

Chris did not laugh, as he was supposed to do. "You don't know me one little bit, Linda Harlan," he accused. "You're right about one thing, though: I won't need a *nurse*. But I'll always need the woman I love — and that's you."

He reached up from his wheel chair and, with lofty disregard for curious onlookers, tried to draw Linda close to him. When she flushed and pulled back, he grinned and said:

"Okay. We have an audience, so we do it your way. Sorry. I didn't mean to embarrass you. It's just that I love you — so why shouldn't the little ol' world know? I'm proud of it."

Linda had no ready answer. As a nurse, she supposed, she should speak sharply to this confused and confusing patient. However, as a woman, she could not bring herself to speak sharply to a man who not only had declared his love but wanted the whole world to know about it.

"Oh, Chris, be sensible," she begged. "Patients do sometimes get ideas like that about their nurses. But it isn't love. It's — well, just a sort of passing affection

160

of the weak for the strong . . . "

Chris stiffened. "I suppose it couldn't work both ways, huh?" he challenged. "Such as a beautiful nurse falling in love with a no-good patient?"

"Well, anyhow," Linda said evasively, "those lovely fantasies never last, never work out."

"Ours could last — that is, if we both work at it, as I aim to do. You seem to forget I'm turning in this buckboard" — Chris indicated the wheel chair — "for shoe leather. Next time you see me, I'll be walking tall, tall, *tall*!"

Linda forced a smile, tried to speak, but could not get the words past the lump in her throat.

"I'll also be grinning fit to kill, knowing my true love will be waiting for me right here. That's a date, huh?"

Again Linda tried to speak. Now was the time to tell him, she reflected; the moment in which to make it clear to Chris that, when he came back, walking — as he surely would — she would not be here, waiting. She would be deep in the rain forests, carrying on with the work she was trained for, meant for.

And yet how to tell him? How to convince him that his need for her was over and done with, while her own need to be needed would continue? Was it absolutely necessary to be cruel in order to be kind?

Then the moment was gone. Christopher Osborne, Senior, accompanied by an attendant, barged into the picture and began wheeling Chris out toward the waiting plane. And so there was time only for a quick goodbye kiss, after which Linda heard herself murmuring such inanities as:

"So long, cowboy — and good luck. Don't forget to keep your boots on, your grin going, your chin up. I'm counting on you to walk tall, tall, *tall*!"

A few minutes later, blinking back the tears, she stood watching the plane take off, become airborne, finally disappearing in the gathering clouds that betokened a long rainy season ahead. Presently, straightening her shoulders, she turned and walked thoughtfully out to the Osbornes' chauffeur-driven limousine that was waiting to take her back to the city.

Her world and Chris' world, she

reflected, had only one thing in common: problems. They were like two out-of-orbit satellites that had collided in space, pausing briefly before moving on. It was time now to move on.

Very soon she would be entering still another world — a world in which sickness, privation and superstition were said to be an accepted way of life. But she had no misgivings. Chris, perhaps without realizing it, had pointed up a rule that made personal courage mandatory: 'Walk tall, tall, *tall*!'

10

IT was April and the rainy season was well under way when, finally, Linda found herself in the rain forests of Central Africa. She had been traveling all day, through increasingly desolate territory and varying degrees of precipitation.

What had started off early in the morning as a seemingly innocuous game of sunshine and showers had escalated into a king-size cloudburst around noontime. By mid-afternoon, the rain had settled into a steady downpour, converting rural bridges into booby traps and country roads into streams of muddy water, made hazardous by hidden potholes and unexpected washouts.

In the more remote sections of the interior, bugaboo walls were being dissolved, thatched huts leveled, while luckless villagers were seeking whatever shelter they could find for themselves, their families and small livestock. Occasional reed huts set up on stilts appeared to be their only refuge.

To Linda, still a stranger to the vagaries of a tropical rainy season and observing for the first time its pitiless invasion on helpless tribespeople, it was a dismal picture. Conditions worsened perceptibly as the muddy Volkswagen in which she was now riding ploughed its way deeper into the bush country.

Since leaving Monrovia around daybreak, she had traveled in all manner of conveyances, including a mammy-wagon. First, there was the Osbornes' chauffeur-driven car, which had been left at her disposal, to the airport. Next, there had been the luxury jet out of Robertsfield, taking her eastward, through Ghana, Nigeria, and on to the last scheduled stop before Leopoldville. Then there was a short, abortive flight in a helicopter sent out by the clinic to meet her, but soon grounded because of poor visibility.

After that, there was a money-bus, which also proved unrainworthy. When the vehicle balked at negotiating a swaying monkey-bridge, Linda had hitched a ride on a market wagon into the nearest village. There, she'd been met by the English-speaking black boy, in the mud-splashed Volkswagen that would take her on to her destination: the health and research center in the province of Marimbia, town of Bugaboo.

"Young Doc, he say I am your boy, missy," the unsmiling African had told her, pronouncing each word with painstaking care. "My name, it is Somali. At the clinic, I am called Sam."

"Thank you, Sam. It's very kind of you to come for me," Linda said with equally careful enunciation. "I am Linda Harlan, a nurse from the States. I am here to help out through the rainy season. Now tell me, what do you do at the clinic besides rescuing ladies in distress?" she queried conversationally.

"Me, I work many hours," the black boy announced gravely. "I study many hours, and I watch. I learn to heal my people — like Young Doc, my boss-man."

"Oh. You mean Dr. Paul Raymond. I'm sure he's a good boss-man and a fine teacher."

The boy nodded agreement, but his solemn demeanor did not alter. "From you, missy, I will also learn to heal my people. I do not burn inside to become a witch doctor like my father and my father's father."

There were no further attempts at conversation, the boy's expression indicating that he preferred silence to small talk. Deftly he had disposed of Linda's traveling bags, helped her into the Volkswagen, climbed in behind the wheel and started the motor. A moment later the sturdy vehicle, veering southward, was entering the last lap of the long, tiresome journey.

Now, less than an hour later, darkness had moved in. The rain was still beating down with businesslike intensity, and the car was obliged to proceed at a snail's pace to avoid washouts. Visibility was rapidly approaching the blackout stage.

Nevertheless, as they passed through several dimly lighted settlements, Linda caught glimpses of shadowy figures moving back and forth, as though dancing. She was aware, too, of eerie background sounds, as of muted tom-toms beating out a dirge-like refrain. She remarked on it, adding:

"I suppose it's native music, but people can't possibly be dancing in a downpour like this. Unless" — she hesitated — "they're the devil-dancers I've read about."

"What you hear, missy, it is drum-talk," the black boy intoned, and buttoned his lips tight against further disclosure.

"Yes, of course. I know about talking drums, devildances and other such pagan rites. But I never expected to hear or see them. They're supposed to mean trouble, aren't they? Or do they drive evil spirits away?"

"Me, I would not know about that, missy." The denial came quickly, stiffly. "It is best not to hear drum-talk. It is best not to see the devils dancc."

Linda caught the inference. Obviously The Rule: 'See nothing, hear nothing, say nothing,' was rigidly observed around here. She would have to be careful.

But she could not *un*-hear the ominous pulsating of drums in the dark, nor *un*-see the weird spectacle of shadowy dancers in the rain. And she could not shake off the feeling that evil and superstition lurked somewhere in the blackness ahead; that the taciturn colored boy at her side knew and feared more than he dared to reveal.

Presently the road widened, became more navigable, and the flickering lights of a sizable village came into view. A group of white stucco buildings emerged out of the rain-swept darkness. They were lit brightly, and a spotlight out front illuminated a sign identifying the oasis as the research and health center.

Also visible, but not spotlighted, was a group of thatched pavilions, now empty, and a cluster of stilt-huts whose small, shuttered windows were closed against the rain. The pavilions, according to the colored boy, Sam, were for patients when weather conditions permitted; the houses, for attendants, trainees and certain other hospital personnel.

"Many sick people," he explained matter-of-factly. "Small-small room for them."

This, then, was her home in the bush, Linda reflected. Quite a contrast to the Harlans' charming oceanside villa, and completely different from the Osbornes' de luxe suite in the Intercontinental.

However, if it had to be a thatched hut in a rain-drenched jungle, she would accept it, walking tall, tall, *tall* . . .

Inside the clinic, she was greeted with friendly warmth by Dr. Paul Raymond and his colleague, Dr. Armstrong. An elderly man with a crest of white hair and kindly brown eyes, the senior doctor beamed his approval.

"You're a beautiful sight for tired eyes, my dear," he commented pleasantly. "And what's more important, you're a full-fledged nurse. I'm in love with you already."

"The feeling is mutual, sir," Linda retorted, pleasantly.

Paul Raymond did not join in the laughter that followed, apparently choosing to reserve judgment. "I didn't realize you were a redhead," he said presently. "However, we shall see what we shall see."

Linda bit back the obvious retort: 'What's my hair got to do with my ability as a nurse? Maybe I don't like your crew cut, either!'

Dr. Paul Raymond, at first glance, was just as she remembered him from the Dakar-Monrovia plane ride. 'Cotton-pickin' hairdo,' as Chris Osborne called the trim crew cut, and gray eyes that were neither too old to twinkle with laughter, nor too young to reflect remembered pain. A man who could be stern, even autocratic, she suspected. Persistent, too, she decided further, recalling his tenacity in getting her there!

It occurred to Linda that Paul Raymond was handsomer than she'd first thought. Or was the change due to the hospital whites, which suited him so perfectly, in contrast to the ill-fitting suit he had worn on the plane? His tall, athletic figure seemed to dominate the clinic, dwarfing that of his associate, though Dr. Armstrong was not a small man. Here, in his rightful environment, there was no evidence of his earlier humility. It was clear that he kowtowed to no one, as Greg Arnold sometimes did for reasons of policy. Nor did he, like Chris Osborne, demand kowtowing from others. He walked tall, almost too tall, setting a pace that might not be easy to follow.

While they ate a simple dinner on a

card table set up in a corridor, the two men told Linda something about the setup. Starting off as a research center for the purpose of combatting tropical diseases in general, malaria in particular, the project had mushroomed to include a free clinic, a small hospital, and even a school for trainees.

"Now," Paul Raymond announced sourly, "we've got a Frankinstein on our hands. The tail, in fact, is wagging the dog."

"Well," Dr. Armstrong explained, "we couldn't turn sick people away. And we couldn't handle the traffic without help, so it was necessary to train our own. One thing led to another . . . "

"See what I mean?" the younger doctor said, "It's one of those vicious circles you hear about. And you can imagine what's happening to Research, Miss Harlan. It's going to pot — fast."

Nervously, Linda looked from one doctor to the other and was relieved to see that the older man was smiling. "Pay no attention to the young whippersnapper, my dear," he said. "Paul is just talking. He'd be the first to object if we so much as turned a case of spavin away. And I'd hate to think what would happen if anybody, even our sponsors, suggested closing the training school. That's Paul's baby. He's even got the Peace Corps donating their time, teaching English."

Paul Raymond calmed down, grinning sheepishly. "We couldn't possibly close our school. What would we use for help? Why, those trainees are not only making it possible for us to carry on here; they are teaching their people, putting the witch doctors out of business."

Later, he showed Linda around the main building, lingering for some time in the well-equipped laboratory, which he admitted was his pride and joy. He also pointed out a group of malaria and bilharzia patients in a small, crowded ward, explaining they were there for observation, tests and other research purposes. Then he briefed Linda on her various duties, admitting frankly that they included just about everything.

The first hundred days would be the hardest, Paul Raymond prophesied. "In a way, it's a blood bath — well, until the worst of the rainy season is over — if we

173

live that long," he qualified — the clinic aimed to start on an expansion program, made possible by a generous donation from Christopher Osborne, Senior.

"Also, we hoped to have help, trained personnel from the States," he went on to say. "Meanwhile, it's a rat race. Think you can take it?"

"I'm pretty durable," Linda assured him.

"Good. Useful as well as ornamental, huh? *That* I'll have to see to believe. It isn't often those two qualities come in the same package," Paul Raymond observed wryly, thus converting what might have been a passing compliment into a challenge.

Much to Linda's relief, she was not assigned to one of the thatched huts outside, designated by Sam as living quarters for the hired help. As the only bona fide, all-purpose nurse on the premises, she was given a comfortable, air-conditioned room in the main building, where she could be available at all times. And promptly at seven o'clock the following morning, her 'blood bath' began.

Her duties, she soon found, were as varied as they were numerous, running the gamut of routine activities, from helping 'Papa Doc,' as the elderly Dr. Armstrong was affectionately called, in surgery, to pinch-hitting for 'Young Doc' in coping with in-and out-patients who spoke a bewildering variety of tribal languages; always with black Sam, who proudly described himself as 'Missy's boy,' on hand to take over any unpleasant details.

There were evenings in the research laboratory with Dr. Paul Raymond, getting to know the various facts concerning tropical diseases — their cause, their treatment, and the problems encountered in seeking a means of control. Evenings only because the daytime hours, for both Paul and herself, were crowded with hospital work. Already the rains had put the outdoor pavilions out of business, reducing space accommodations to a minimum; now it was raining patients, overtaxing all available facilities, and prodding working personnel into frenzied activity.

Research was suffering in proportion.

The search for the elusive ounce of prevention was losing out to the more pressing task of administering the equally elusive pound of cure. In fact, the battle against tropical diseases was getting nowhere.

There were rewarding interludes spent in small classrooms where young tribespeople, reputedly descendants of cannibals, were learning English under the tutelage of Peace Corps volunteers. They were studying practical nursing, midwivery, first aid, and the rudiments of medical science. The object being, each and every one of them would say, as though repeating a theme song:

'To help my people.'

Linda was touched. Some of these trainees, she reflected, would remain there, working as orderlies, attendants, aides. Others would go deeper into the rain forests, ministering as best they could to the needs of their tribespeople. Still others, the idealistic ones such as Sam, would find a way to continue their training, perhaps in Monrovia, Europe, or even America, to return as full-fledged doctors.

"I'll see to it that Sam gets his chance," she promised herself as she watched her loyal helper go about his duties with silent efficiency.

She made a mental note to write to Christopher Osborne, Senior, about this earnest black boy, the confessed son of a witch doctor, whose dream was to become a bona fide physician — 'like Young Doc, my bossman.' Later, when she returned to the States, she would enlist Greg Arnold's help on behalf of Sam.

Oh, yes, she had answered Greg's letters; could return to Riverview any time she chose to work on the new research program either as Gregory Arnold's teammate or his bride. She had made no commitments. It would do the self-assured young man no harm to stew in his own juice for a while, she'd decided.

And so the days passed, sultry and rain-swept and problem-ridden. They lengthened into weeks; weeks in which nerves became taut and frustration was an ever-present specter. As Paul Raymond had prophesied, it was indeed a blood bath.

Nevertheless, everyone was taking it in stride, with a kind of patient gallantry that was contagious. Under the circumstances, Linda was not finding it too difficult to keep up the pace. The work, while exhausting, was stimulating, sometimes exciting, and the hundred hardest days were passing.

April and May had been washed out of existence, and June was floating in. The remaining month would pass just as certainly. Once the rainy season was over, Linda felt she could get on with her personal life, at peace with her conscience and all the more competent as a nurse for this unique experience.

Moreover, all was not work. There was a time for relaxation — a health 'must' for Americans living in tropical Africa. Every now and then, at the insistence of the two doctors, Linda would join the local Peace Corps volunteers in what they called a 'Saturday-night fun-fest,' said to be a safeguard against 'freaking out.'

Once a week, the celebrants would travel by jeep or Volkswagen, or on foot, through the rain to a school-house they'd built with their hands, which served as a meeting place, chanting, tongue in cheek:

"It's not raining rain, you know; it's raining love and stuff."

It was clear that each and every one of these young crusaders knew very well that the prolonged rainy season was doing strange things to human emotions, their own as well as those of the tribespeople. There were rumors of unrest among the natives, but due to the hush-hush policy that prevailed in all of Africa, they had no choice other than to concentrate on their own nostalgic malcontent.

Gathered together in the jerry-built schoolhouse, they would try to drown out the rain with gay conversation, high laughter, music and song; and facetious reminiscences of a homeland that seemed so far away as to be nebulous. Meanwhile, they would nibble on sodden pretzels and hard-as-nails cookies, washing them down with sips of palm wine that smelled to high heaven and tasted like gasoline.

Presently someone would dig up a guitar whose strings were still intact but whose box had been badly damaged by driver's ants. And they would sing all the songs — old and new — that they could remember, raising their voices to incredible heights, as if by doing so they could torment the evil spirits into making the rain go away.

Inevitably, at this point, some homesick rookie, female variety, would burst into tears. Just as inevitably, a bearded youth wearing faded jeans and barefoot sandals would saunter over, presumably to comfort her, and an amorous scene would ensue.

"It's the rain, honey," someone would murmur in response to Linda's gasp. "It does things to the emotions. Just wait. You'll see."

Whereupon a tape recorder would be turned on, and the evening would proceed with seemly propriety, under the cooling influence of hot music and frenzied modern dancing.

Despite his elderly associate's insistence that all work and no play was the bane of the medical profession, Paul Raymond never joined in these friendly get-togethers. Which was just as well, Linda decided, though there were times when she, as the only loner in the group, felt lost without an escort.

However, there was no gainsaying the fact that Paul Raymond lacked the *savoir faire* of Boston-bred Greg Arnold and had none of the reckless gayety characteristic of Chris Osborne. Unlike the other Saturday-night celebrants, he could not — or *would* not — let himself go.

Moreover, he was not one to mince words. He would be quick to say that he wanted no part in such 'crackpot immaturity,' as he would label the innocent fun explosion. In fact, he would make it embarrassingly clear that he much preferred to be back at the clinic with his microscope, snails and mosquitoes.

They'd heckle him — the nitwits! — and I couldn't bear that, Linda told herself, her heart touched with compassion for this dedicated medical man who was working so earnestly against odds.

It occurred to her that, as time passed, Paul Raymond was coming to rely on her more and more, seemingly oblivious to the fact that, come the dry season, she would be leaving. She supposed she should remind him that the current arrangement was only temporary. But somehow she could not bring herself to do so. In a way, it would be like a slap in the face of his unfulfilled dreams. Whereas she was free to leave the dreary rain forest, to go wherever she chose, he was stuck there until such time as he could come up with something of value to Research.

Oh, well, at least I'm a good influence, she assured herself smugly. He's calmed down a whole lot since I came here, though he has every reason to be disheartened.

What she did not suspect was that the harassed young doctor's apparent calm was brewing up a massive storm. Therefore, she was genuinely surprised when, on a sultry July evening, Paul Raymond's frustration exploded into words that no dedicated humanitarian in his right mind would utter. They were in the laboratory working on what he sometimes described as 'non-progress reports for armchair scientists in the States,' when he impaled Linda with rebellious gray eyes and all but shouted:

"What the devil am I doing here?" He

answered his own question: "Running myself and everybody else ragged; trying to be all things to all sick people, while the work I ought to be doing goes to pot."

"Well," Linda said, taken aback by this outburst, "aren't doctors *supposed* to be all things to all sick people?"

"This is *supposed* to be a research center; not a schoolhouse, an all-purpose hospital, an aid to the population explosion. Now just look at us! How the heck did it happen?"

Linda tried for a lighter note. "Oh, come now, Dr. Raymond. You're just pooped, out of sorts. You know very well how it happened. It happened because you're a doctor, and dedicated. You wouldn't have it any other way. Oh, I know you're discouraged, but I can't see you letting a sick person down."

"The name is Paul," he corrected. "Good old Paul, the perennial patsy, always on hand with his stethoscope, from the first bawl to the last gasp. Dedicated? Heck, if I never see another sick person, it will be a whole lot too soon."

Linda was not deceived. "Pooh yourself, Paul. There will always be sick people needing help. And there will always be Pauls to help them. And Gregs," she added softly.

Paul Raymond only smiled wryly and said, "Thanks for the vote of confidence. Now, shall we get on with the show? It's pushing nine-thirty, and these reports should go out tomorrow, weather permitting."

For two hours they worked in the laboratory, speaking only in terms of tropical diseases, their origin, their increasing prevalence in defiance of wonder drugs, and the chances of an early breakthrough in control.

Grateful that there were no interruptions, Paul sat bent over microscope and charts, pinpointing the habits of the Anopheles mosquito, the tsetse fly and other killer parasites endemic to the tropics. Meanwhile Linda, drooping from fatigue, was taking notes for a comprehensive progress report.

There was another half-hour spent with victims of malaria, sleeping sickness and similar ailments. There they examined charts, checking on patients' reactions to various treatments, finally returning to the laboratory to complete the master reports.

Presently, with an impatient gesture, Paul Raymond pushed his paper work aside to fasten uncompromising eyes upon his unsuspecting helper.

"Who the devil is this Greg-person you're forever talking about?" he demanded abruptly. "Somebody I'm supposed to know?"

A telltale flush spread across Linda's face. The chart and pencil she was holding fell to the floor with an unreasonably loud clatter. For the life of her, she could not recall having mentioned Greg's name in front of Paul Raymond.

"No — uh — no," she stammered. "It isn't likely you'd know Gregory Arnold. He — well, he's somebody I knew back at Riverview, in Boston. Funny thing," she babbled on, unable to stop herself, "he's getting interested in research on tropical diseases, the kind you're doing. Quite a coincidence, don't you think?"

Paul Raymond shook his head. No, there was nothing funny, nothing coincidental, about that, he pointed out. A lot of young medicos were training for research, now that so many service men were being assigned to tropical areas. "I understand more hospital beds are filled with Malaria patients than with men wounded in action," he declared. "Aside from girls, it's all the troops talk about."

"Yes, so I've heard. Riverview is adding a new wing especially for tropical research."

"Good. Now back to that Greg character — couldn't we get him over here? We have all the ingredients for compulsive research — straight through from the culprit to the corpse. We could well use more help, another trainee."

Linda wrung her hands in distress. "Oh, please, Paul, you don't understand. Greg isn't just a trainee."

"What is he then? Until we get this thing licked, we're all trainees."

"He's an M.D., one of the finest. You couldn't possibly expect a person of Gregory Arnold's stature to come into a miserable rain forest like this."

"Why not, for Pete's sake?" Paul exploded. "I'm an M.D., and I'm here.

You said he's interested in research on tropical diseases, didn't you? Or did I misunderstand that, too?"

"No. You're right," Linda conceded. "He's enormously interested. According to the grapevine, he's to be assigned to the hospital's new research project, maybe as one of the top men."

"You don't say. Then that's all the more reason he should come to this miserable rain forest," Paul snapped. "He may get his pinfeathers damp, but he'll soak up a lot of know-how he won't find in books. That's for sure."

Linda took refuge in enthusiasm for the absent one, endowing Gregory Arnold with all the virtures she could dream up at the moment. He was not only a wonderful doctor, a wonderful friend, but a wonderful man, she avowed.

"Oh. So it's like that," her listener commented dryly. "You're in love with the creep."

Linda neither confirmed nor denied the charge. She sat silent, listening to the rain beating down on the tin roof, wishing the world would stop moving long enough for her to get off.

"I won't embarrass you by asking how come you ran away from this remarkable specimen," Paul was saying. "That's understandable. It's no picnic keeping step with hard-shell perfection. What I can't figure out is this: how could any man in his right mind let a wonderful girl like you escape? If he'd had the sense of a half-wit, he'd have locked you up."

Perversely, Linda returned to her defense of Gregory Arnold. "You don't need to be sarcastic. You've got Greg all wrong. He's much too busy for romantic detours, because — well, his life isn't his own."

"You don't say?"

"Yes. I do say. What I mean is — well, his profession comes first, as it should. You know, his solemn oath and all that sort of thing," Linda finished lamely.

Paul Raymond's response was shockingly blunt. He laughed, actually *laughed!*

"What's so funny?" Linda demanded hotly. "You know as well as I do that a doctor's first obligation is to his profession, the humanities. His oath is inviolate and — " She stopped, unable to find words with which to finish the sentence.

"Now I've heard everything." Dr. Paul Raymond chuckled. "I've known all along that the medical profession demands a whole lot of its disciples, but I've never heard tell of a celibacy rule. This, my mixed-up darling, is news!"

11

WHEN Linda's hurt expression did not change, Paul rose to his feet and held out a penitent hand. "Forgive me. I don't know why I'd say such a contemptible thing. Could be I'm a little prejudiced."

"A *little*?" Linda managed a wan smile. "Could be it's rain-fever. Besides, we're both bone-tired. Anyhow, it doesn't matter. I said a lot of foolish things, too."

"What do *you* know about rain-fever?" Paul demanded, looking at Linda sharply. "That's another term for casual sex in this neck of the woods. And it *does* matter, what I said. I've hurt you — the last thing I'd ever want to do. I'm sure your friend Dr. Arnold, the pride of Riverview, is as fine a person as you think he is, but — " Aware of the sarcasm in his voice, he stopped short.

"Well" — Linda hesitated — "Greg does have a few faults; no one is absolutely perfect." Desperately, she tried for a laugh, saying with self-conscious absurdity, "Riverview isn't exactly a monastery."

"No. It isn't exactly a convent either, I suspect." Paul thought a minute, then said with seeming irrelevance:

"I've always told myself there's no percentage in being the first man in a girl's life; it's being the last one that counts. It's unreasonable to assume that a sweetheart like you could have escaped love. And only an utter fool would start dissecting his blessings." He broke off to say with some resentment:

"Well, it looks like I'm that kind of a fool, darling. I'm in love with you, so I'm jealous of anybody and everybody you ever knew."

Before Linda could challenge his peculiarly masculine assumption that love begat love, there was a knock on the door. An instant later Sam entered the laboratory full of apologies and announcing in a perturbed voice that there were patients in the clinic. His face registered concern, and he appeared to be having difficulty with his English.

"I am sorry," he droned. "The clock, she say it is much late, and Papa Doc, he is sleeping. But they travel in much rain. So I do not say, 'Go home, tribespeople.'"

Paul Raymond muttered something to the effect that Fate and the medical profession had entered into a conspiracy to frustrate any dreams he might have of marital happiness. Aloud, he said kindly to the colored boy:

"That's right, Sam. Never tell sick people to go home. Many of these poor devils have been rained out of their homes," he said in an aside to Linda. "But don't start asking what we'll use for beds. We'll put straw pallets here in the laboratory or somewhere."

Sam's dark face shone with gratitude, but his eyes remained apprehensive. "A tribesman name of Kali, he is here. He bring with his woman, name of Zalina, a small small baby, and the placenta. Kali, he is my friend. I tell him to come here. They do not ask for beds."

Both doctor and nurse were relieved to hear that they were merely facing a routine task. Sometimes a new father, having delivered his own baby, would bring the placenta in for examination instead of throwing it out to the jackals. It was a practice, a precaution, followed by awakening tribespeople as old customs gave way to modern medical science. Remote tribesmen were heeding warnings against possible infection, just as their wives were beginning to realize that pure water and sanitation had some connection with health.

"The small small baby, he does not look sick," Sam was saying. "But Zalina, the woman" — he hesitated, swallowed hard, and his eyes bugged — "she is wearing the charm. Witch doctor, he tell her small baby has devil inside. Zalina, she buy charm to send evil spirits away"

"Never mind the charm, Sam," Paul said. "You know very well those fetishes mean nothing."

"And there are no such things as evil spirits and devil babies," Linda pointed out.

"Yes, missy, I know. But Kali's woman, she not know. Maybe she go back to witch doctor, and maybe small baby must die!"

"That's enough, Sam," Paul warned. "Now go back and tell them I'll be right out. And you're not to listen to any further talk about charms and devils and witch doctors. Understand?"

"Yessir, Boss," Sam promised, and hurried back to the clinic.

With the same speed with which he had stepped out of the role of potential lover into that of kindly employer, Paul Raymond became the working doctor. Going over to a sink, he washed his hands carefully in filtered water, slipped into his white jacket and, without so much as a glance in Linda's direction, turned to leave the laboratory.

Linda, with matching impersonality, rose from her chair, the dutiful nurse. "I'll go for you, Dr. Raymond. I can handle the situation. Don't forget morning comes early; you have those reports to finish — and another hard day in front of you."

"No, I'll go." Paul smiled. "I'm no tireder than you are. Never mind tomorrow. We'll face that together."

"Then we'll both go." Linda studied her wrist watch through fatigue-glazed eyes. "Tomorrow is already here."

When she entered the clinic, only a few paces behind Paul, Linda saw nothing amiss about the tableau that came into view. The young tribesman named Kali — tall and straight and ebony black — stood holding an ornately decorated bowl containing the placenta. Although his clothes were dripping wet, he had managed to protect the bowl and its contents from the downpour.

A young woman sat on one of the outpatient benches, breast-feeding an infant. She was wearing a colorfully patterned lappa whose enveloping folds all but concealed the baby in her arms. Obviously she was trying not to see the bedeviled child. A makeshift tarpaulin, reinforced by palm fronds, lay at her feet, mute evidence that she and her small bundle from heaven — or wherever — had been carefully protected from the elements.

Meanwhile Sam, as far removed as possible from the contaminating scene, stood awaiting orders. Apparently having recovered his aplomb to some extent, he was having no further truck with benighted fellow-tribes-people who still believed in witch doctors, fetishes and long-gone evil spirits.

Drawing nearer, however, Linda became aware of an ominous tenseness as two pairs of frightened dark eyes — Kali's and Zalina's — darted from doctor to nurse, finally coming to rest upon the infant at its mother's breast. Sam, too, appeared to be having a slight relapse into the area of superstition. His eyes were bugging again, and when he opened his lips to speak, nothing came out.

Curious to see the talisman that was supposed to have magic powers over devils, mortal and/or immortal, Linda focused her attention on the woman. All she saw in the way of a charm was a necklace fashioned of chacha seeds, from which dangled an oversized pendant that challenged closer inspection. It looked like a melange of animal teeth, matted feathers and birds' claws.

Linda had seen other native women wearing similar ornaments and had marveled at the weird ingenuity expressed in tribal art. Up until now it had not occurred to her that such baubles might have a diabolical meaning. She wondered if the unfortunate baby was wearing one of the evil things and winced at the thought.

"I'm getting goose pimples all over," she whispered to Paul, who appeared to be the only unperturbed person in the room. "Why, this girl's scared to death of her own baby. She wouldn't kill it, would she?"

"Certainly not," Paul answered cheerfully. Impassively, he went about the routine matter of checking on the placenta, pronounced it intact, and ordered Sam to dispose of it.

"Be sure to bring the bowl back," he told the boy. "I've a feeling our good friends, Kali and Zalina, will be needing it again. Something tells me little Snoozer here" — he inclined his head toward the infant, now sleeping peacefully — "is the first in a long line of fine youngsters." He motioned to Linda, saying:

"We'll take them back to the exam room for a check-up, though we'll have to play it in pantomime till Sam rejoins us. Communication problems. There are hundreds of dialects in these parts;

impossible to learn them all."

"I wish this was only a communication problem," Linda murmured. "It isn't that simple."

Paul caught her arm and pressed it gently. "Don't look so woebegone, honey. We aren't here to Westernize these people. We are only trying to help them. It takes time to overcome centuries of superstition, and time is one of the commodities we don't have too much of around here. In this case, Mama's been seeing too many witch doctors, but Papa's beginning to see daylight. It will all turn out right in the end."

"I hope so."

Discouraged but not defeated by the language barrier, the ill-assorted group fled out of the clinic in a kind of stoical silence. Paul Raymond, looking confident as you please, led the way, followed by a bewildered father and a terrified mother, who were holding hands like lost children in an unexplored forest.

Linda, walking behind them, looked down at the cunning baby boy she was carrying in her arms and sighed. The infant, awake now, stared back at her, his solemn black eyes eloquent with silent appeal. Impulsively she drew him closer, as if by doing so she could express the compassion in her heart.

She wished she could share Paul's optimism as to the outcome of this case. But somehow she could not. She recalled stories about babies who had died at the hands of their parents, innocent victims of superstitious fear. Although Zalina and her child were pronounced physically sound, she was relieved to see that arrangements were being made to keep the two at the clinic overnight.

Sam rounded up several trainees who lived in the huts on the premises. A bed was set up in a corridor for the mother, a cushioned reed basket for the baby, and they were made comfortable for what was left of the night. Almost immediately they were asleep; the baby, unaware of the evil role to which an itinerant witch doctor had assigned him, slumbering peacefully, the mother clinging fast to the ugly talisman.

"Are you *sure* they'll be all right?" Linda prodded when she and Paul were back in the laboratory. "Don't you think

I should take my paper work and sit there? Or maybe take the infant into my room where it will be safe?"

"Certainly I'm sure." A sharpness had crept into the harassed doctor's voice, and he frowned with impatience. "And most certainly you are *not* going to sit there, or take the child into your room. How screwy can you get?"

"How heartless can *you* get?" Linda retorted, and resolved then and there to keep an eye on the obsessed mother — never mind Dr. Paul Raymond. "Unreasonable, too," she tacked on for good measure.

"I can be pretty heartless when my back is against the wall," Paul said with a stiffness that should have warned Linda. "I'm responsible for this operation. I refuse to have the place turned upside down just because a couple of pixillated natives barge in after midnight with a baby that might better have remained unborn. What's so unreasonable about that?"

"You really can be hardhearted, can't you?" Linda flung back. "Why, when I think of those poor bewildered people, especially that helpless baby, I could bawl . . . " Her voice broke, and her eyes swam with tears of exhaustion.

Paul Raymond, his gray eyes bleak with frustration, ran an impatient hand through his crew cut. "Control yourself, Nurse Harlan," he reproved her with a show of authority. "Let us not get hysterical. Remember: a first-class nurse never indulges in nerves. We are doing all we can for the tribespeople around here."

It was a rebuke well deserved, Linda conceded privately. But her resentment flared into anger when Sam's murmured, "Yes, missy, we does what we can" revealed the presence of an audience.

She wished she could forget the iron-clad rule about nurse-doctor relationships and give Dr. Paul Raymond a piece of her mind. More than anything, she wanted to say quite impertinently: "First-class doctors do not belittle R.N.'s in front of the hired help."

On the other hand, she supposed she should forgive the offender on the grounds that he was over-tired, overworked, and understandably discouraged because his plans for research were being balked on all sides. But then, so was she over-tired, overworked, and discouraged because circumstances were making it impossible to follow the rules consistent with first-class nursing.

Since back talk was not a working nurse's prerogative, it gave her some satisfaction to agree with Sam when, chancing the doctor's disfavor, he took it upon himself to suggest that the revolting fetish be taken away from the sleeping tribeswoman.

"Witchcraft, she is bad medicine," the colored boy said, virtuously repeating a memorized line. "Me, I burn inside to take thc cvil charm away while Zalina sleep."

"I wish you would," Linda exclaimed. "The very sight of that dreadful thing makes my flesh crawl. Teeth, feathers, claws — ugh!"

Sam nodded his head vigorously. "Yes, missy. The charm, she stinks. She, like a placenta, is for the jackals. She is not good for woman with small small baby."

Paul Raymond groaned aloud. "Oh,

for gosh sake, couldn't we forget that charm business for now? Must we make a thing of it? It's only a symbol and will do the girl no harm. Couldn't we just leave it at that?"

"No. We can't leave it at that," Linda announced stubbornly. "At least *I* can't." She knew she was sticking her neck out, but at this point she was beyond caring. "The charm can do a whole lot of harm, emotionally. It might give her ideas. Why, I couldn't sleep a wink worrying about what she might do to that poor baby."

"Okay, okay, Sam, take the blasted thing away," Paul bellowed. He made a gesture of dismissal, and the colored boy left the room. Then, in a gentler tone, to Linda:

"Nothing's going to happen to our little black cherub. He's as sound as a new dollar. In six months he'll be crawling into his elegant ancestral stool; it'll be covered with tiger skin and dripping fine beads. He'll be the grandest tiger in the jungle. You'll see."

Linda was not reassured. Oh, she had heard all about the elaborate ceremonial chairs presented to male off-spring who were favored by the gods; destined to live and to vanquish all foes, mortal and immortal. It was a pretty superstition, but somehow she could not visualize such good fortune for the offspring of a woman so possessed by black magic as to fear the fruit of her own womb. She could only murmur shakily, as she had before:

"I hope you're right, Dr. Raymond."

"Well, right or wrong, there's not much we can do at the moment. Doing away with a charm solves nothing. Mama can always get another one, if she knows the right witch doctor — and apparently she does."

All of which made sense to Linda. She started to say so, but the doctor's next remark brought an angry flush to her face, and her resentment flared anew.

"Are you sure *you* don't believe in witchcraft, Miss Harlan? I'm beginning to suspect the ol' conjure man's digging you too."

"Certainly I'm not superstitious. But — but — " Tears of vexation welled up in Linda's eyes.

"You don't want to tempt Fate, huh? Okay. A bewitched medic hasn't a chance against the fatal charm of a beautiful, teary-eyed nurse."

The doctor's indulgent smile did not remove the sting from his words. Then, his eyes twinkling momentarily, he added what, to Linda, was the final straw:

"Want to wear the official wig, honey?" With a quick gesture, he made as though to remove his crew cut and place it upon his outraged nurse's head. Linda stiffened and said coldly:

"Are you, by any chance, suggesting that I change my profession, Dr. Raymond, since I'm such a washout as a nurse? Or would you prefer that I change myself? In either case, you're wasting your precious time."

The twinkle went out of Paul's eyes; he stepped over to stand beside Linda and laid a hand on her arm. She tried to inch away from him, but his grasp tightened.

"Look here now," he said; "let's not fight. We're both on edge, saying things we don't mean. If I said something wrong — "

"You didn't. That's what makes me so mad," Linda confessed. "You're so right I could scream. To tell the truth, you're getting more like Greg Arnold every day!"

"Oh." Paul's quick flush gave way to a sour grin. "Am I supposed to feel flattered? Sorry — I don't. What do you mean, I'm getting to be like that so-and-so?"

"Well" — Linda hesitated, then plunged ahead — "expecting a nurse to be as perfect as you are; making her feel guilty if she doesn't measure up. You don't need to remind me that a nurse, like a doctor, is strictly for healing; supposed to have no emotions, no feelings at all . . . "

"Whoa there," Paul broke in. "If that's a rule for medics, I'm afraid I wouldn't qualify. Where the heck did you get that crazy idea? But never mind telling me. I can guess. Who says you aren't perfect?"

"I do. But I can't change myself. I've tried." Linda, all of the fight gone out of her, spoke in a tight little voice that was all but lost in the sound of rain beating down on the tin roof.

"I love nursing; it's my life," she rushed on breathlessly. "But I can't seem to conform with the personality rules. I can never see a patient — even a voodooed tribeswoman — as just another case. And I always die a little when a single thing goes wrong. That's how imperfect I am." She squeezed back the tears, took a deep breath and continued sturdily:

"You'd think I didn't know the first thing about nurse-patient relationships, wouldn't you? I'm forever getting emotionally involved, going overboard. I'm impulsive, overly sympathetic, sentimental . . . "

"And stubborn, too, honey child; don't forget that," Paul contributed, reverting to his native deep-South drawl. "Obstinate as a little ol' muley calf we used to have down home."

Linda frowned. She had not expected such ready agreement. "All right," she said a little sharply. "So I'm stubborn. Just name any fault inconsistent with good nursing, and I've got it."

"Anyhow, you're efficient, Miss Harlan."

Paul spoke with an exaggerated brusqueness that betrayed his own agitation. "But you're going to be hurt many times, if you keep on taking other people's misfortunes to heart."

"I know that. I'll have to take the hurts. I can't change into an automaton and still live with myself. Want to make something of that, too, Dr. Raymond?" Linda tacked on defiantly.

Paul's immediate answer was an inscrutable smile. Then, without warning, he did a most unethical thing, making a complete shambles of what Linda considered a primary rule in doctor-nurse relationships. Bending over, he pressed his lips against her hair; his arms went around her, hard and assured, as though they belonged there.

"Don't try to change yourself, my beloved," he whispered. "Stay as human and as lovable as you are right now. From where I stand, your imperfections make you perfect."

"Wh — why, Dr. Raymond! What a ridiculous thing to say," Linda gasped. She tried to release herself, but his arms enfolded her closer, closer.

"Shush, darling. I'll admit that was a corny way to say it. But I'm a little on the human side myself." His lips, seeking, found hers, lingered there for a long, intoxicating moment.

Linda had removed her nurse's cap upon re-entering the laboratory. Her red-gold hair shone like an aura in the brilliant glow of the research lamps. But the bright lights also pointed up the telltale flush on her face as she realized, to her dismay, that she did not want to move away from Paul's encircling arms or to evade his hungry kiss.

Never before had she been so conscious of herself as a woman; a woman desired, and — yes — desiring. Only this was the wrong time, the wrong place, the wrong man!

It's this endless rain that's wearing me down, she defended herself privately. This strange isolation gives me the wanton feeling that I am the only woman in the world, Paul Raymond the only man, and nothing else matters. It can't possibly be love. If it's rain-fever, as they call it, I'm having no part of it.

Apparently Paul Raymond was also

having some difficulty justifying the extraordinary performance in his own eyes. Abruptly, he released Linda and stepped back several paces.

"This has gone far enough, Nurse Harlan," he said in a husky voice, and glared at her as though she were the offender. "I'm sorry. I forgot myself. I assure you, it will not happen again."

Feeling that insult was being added to injury, Linda announced hotly, "It certainly won't happen again. Forgot yourself — indeed! Now really, Dr. Raymond, how naïve do you think I am? I hate you!"

"I don't think you're naïve at all. To me, you're special. I think you're wonderful. And in spite of the todo you're making, I refuse to believe you hate me. But we'll have to cool it, for now . . . " Paul paused, evidently expecting further back talk. When there was none, he continued, now speaking in a normal tone of voice:

"This, my darling, is no time for a marriage proposal, no place for a love scene. Right now, I have nothing to offer the woman I love except problems, promises and hopes. Until I come up with something of value to research — and I will one of these days — I'm a complete dud, matrimonially speaking."

"Oh, I wouldn't say that," Linda consoled him, weakening momentarily.

"You don't need to say it. I know." Paul paused again, grinning sheepishly. "Meanwhile, I promise not to crowd you. From here on, I'll keep my greedy eyes and hot hands on the microscope. After all, you don't really know me except as a mosquito-watcher and medical jack-of-all-trades."

In the interest of accepted ethics, Linda felt she had to say something more to express her disapproval of her co-worker's earlier lapse. "You don't know me either; otherwise you'd have realised — " She stopped, and her face crimsoned. In her perturbation, she had almost added that grandmother of all absurd clichés: "I'm not *that* kind of a girl."

"I love you, Linda Harlan," Paul said simply. "That's all I need to know."

Well, it's not all I need to know, Linda thought. Things were happening too suddenly, too fast. She respected, even admired, Paul Raymond as a doctor, a human being, a friend. But was this thing that was happening to her love? Or was it rain-fever in its most virulent form? It was impossible to tell, what with her heart saying one thing, her head another, and the rain against the roof now beating out a deceptively bell-like rhythm.

"We've got a beautiful thing going, honey," Paul was saying. "Let's not spoil it by pulling it apart to see what it's made of. It is not rain-fever, if that's what you're thinking. That's only a side-effect, and intermittent. Love is the beautiful sum of all its wonderful parts. It takes the real article to withstand the acid test of an African rainy season — and ours will, if we work at it"

With that, Paul Raymond, M.D., moved over to his desk, ready to resume his work.

"Now get going, sleepyhead," he said. "Don't just stand there until another problem crops up. You've had a rugged day and must get some shut-eye. That, my beloved, is an order."

There would be other problems tomorrow, and tomorrow, he reminded

Linda. Meanwhile, she was not to worry about a single thing. She was to forget progress reports, voodoo charms, bewitched mothers and bedeviled babies. He would put an aide on watch so that nothing would go wrong, he promised.

"Now, you distracting little witch, will you get going?" he barked. "Or do I have to carry you out bodily and tuck you in bed?"

Linda, her face crimson, turned and got going.

12

LINDA had not expected to sleep much, if at all. Exhausted though she was, she had gone to bed reasonably certain that she would lie awake tossing and turning till daybreak, mulling over the events of the past several hours.

Instead, she must have fallen asleep the instant her head touched the pillow. Unaccountably, it was an untroubled, dreamless sleep, having no conscious beginning and brought to an abrupt end by an eerie combination of sounds: the distant rumble of talking drums whose dirge-like rhythm proclaimed trouble, the splash of rain on the roof, and a nervous tapping on the bedroom door. It was full daylight, and the clock on the bedside table pointed to the unreasonable hour of ten.

"Good grief," Linda groaned. "I was supposed to be on duty at seven." Springing to her feet, she slipped into robe and slippers, clutched wildly at her hair, and called an apologetic "Come in."

A colored girl wearing the blue smock of a trainee entered the room, a troubled look on her face. "Good morning, please, Missy," she said in careful English. "The hour, she is much late."

"You're telling *me*?" Linda retorted, snappish in her exasperation. "Why hasn't someone called me before? Where is everybody? Is something wrong?"

The last question was purely experimental. Linda knew very well that something was wrong. But how to get the details out of a girl whose tribal instincts and upbringing precluded the bearing of news — especially bad news — to a white foreigner?

No, nothing was wrong, the girl avowed, as expected. Dr. Raymond, she said, had given orders that missy was not to be disturbed. "Young Doc, he say you much tired, must rest. Me, I go now. The tribeswoman, Zalina, she is gone."

"Gone?" Taken aback by this news, Linda flailed out with a volley of questions: Where had Zalina gone? Why? When? How? Wasn't it still raining like crazy? Did Dr. Raymond know? Then, when there was no answer beyond a few garbled words:

"Don't just stand there, mumbling double talk and saying nothing is wrong. What exactly has happened?"

The trainee, helpless against the barrage of questions, wrung her hands in distress. Obviously, she was not consciously making double talk. In a language still unfamiliar to her, she was trying earnestly to explain to a white unbeliever an act of heresy that she herself found too dreadful to contemplate:

A magic charm had been stolen from the helpless mother of a devil-possessed child. And the offender was Sam, her romantic idol and fellow-tribesman. The gods would avenge!

As patiently as she could, Linda listened to a hesitant and somewhat sketchy account of what had happened while she slept. Sam, it seemed, had removed the charm from the sleeping tribeswoman and thrown it out to the jackals. Zalina, upon awakening, had threatened to inform the paramount chief of the misdemeanor.

Around daybreak, as if some mighty spirit had summoned them, a group of Zalina's relatives had arrived in a mammy-wagon. She had gone away with them, announcing her intention of putting a conjure on Sam and buying a new charm. She had even taken a lock of Sam's hair for the conjuring, having pulled it out by the roots!

"Young Doc, he say let her go if she want to go," the girl finished. "He want no palawa, he say."

That made sense, Linda conceded. The last thing the clinic wanted was an argument with the natives of their host country. There was unrest everywhere, the world over. And in this highly volatile culture that was the burgeoning Africa, there were invisible lines that discreet foreigners did not cross. As Paul Raymond often pointed out, the clinic's job was to minister to sick bodies, not to ride herd on helpless, tradition-bound souls.

What did not make sense was the continuing rumble of talking drums, the rattle of beads against gourds, punctuated now and then by what sounded precisely like the wail of a stricken animal. Surely a thing as trivial as a missing charm — ugly, smelly, worthless — did not warrant such fanfare. It was nothing more than a coincidence. Linda started to say so, but the troubled look on the black girl's face sent her imagination spiraling, and a new fear gripped her heart.

It came to her in a flash that not once in her halting recital had the trainee mentioned the whereabouts of the supposedly bedeviled baby. Was it safe — alive? Or had the bewitched mother, in panic, contrived to destroy the infant — here in a place where the right to live was inviolate? In that case, there was ample reason for drum talk!

Suddenly Linda had to know the truth, however ugly it might be. "The baby?" She demanded. "Did Zalina leave it here? Is it all right — alive?"

"The baby? You mean the small small baby?"

"Certainly. You heard me. Do I have to spell it out? How dumb can you get?" Linda stormed, reckless in her growing

218

anxiety. "Answer me, black girl! Is that baby dead?" She all but choked over the last word, but she had to say it. "A sacrifice to the whims of your miserable gods?"

Linda knew that she had stumbled across the forbidden line, but in this moment of anxiety she was beyond caring. There was too much at stake to play word games with a stubbornly uncommunicative trainee. In the event of infanticide within its none too sturdy walls, the clinic was doomed. Its absentee sponsors, oblivious to the power of centuries-old susperstition, would abandon the whole project. And Paul's cherished dream of on-the-spot research would be dismissed as just another noble experiment that hadn't worked.

Poor Paul, her heart wept silently. There goes his dream of success. There goes my dream, too, because his dreams are mine, always will be. Aloud she said again, "Answer me, black girl," and steeled herself as best she could against whatever bad news might follow.

The native girl, hurt, flinched visibly. "There is nothing more to tell, Missy," she hedged. "The small small baby, it is not dead." Zalina, a proud tribeswoman, had taken her baby with her, naturally, she announced stiffly, the inference being that proud tribeswomen did not leave their offspring in the hands of godless white foreigners. There was nothing wrong with the infant that a new charm would not fix. Any witch doctor would supply that for a price.

Linda, momentarily relieved, let it go at that. "Then why are the drums talking? What are they saying? Does it have anything to do with the clinic? I never heard such a to-do."

"Drums?" The word was scarcely more than a whisper, and the chocolate-brown eyes widened with fear. "It is best not to hear drums, Missy; best not to know what they are saying. They speak no ill of the clinic."

"Good. Then we have nothing to worry about. Now, if you'll run along, I'll get dressed and on the job. Thank you for calling me. I'm sorry I was cross. I didn't mean to be hateful."

"It is all right." The girl tried to smile, but the desolate look in her eyes remained, prompting Linda to say with sympathetic concern:

"What is it, Ngala? Can't you tell me what's wrong? Maybe I could help. If you're worried about Sam's doing away with the charm — forget it. That was my fault. I told him it gave me the creeps. If there's any trouble, I'll take the blame."

For a moment Ngala stood silent; her chin trembled and her eyes swam with tears. "Nothing is wrong," she reiterated presently. "It is not for Sam that I worry. It is for all my people. The gods, they are mad at us . . . " She started to say more, then shook her head, murmuring, "I go now please, Missy," and left the room, sobbing softly.

Linda, watching her go, felt suspended between pity, frustration and utter helplessness. There was no gainsaying the fact that trouble hovered over the rain forests. But the traditional black curtain was being drawn against the curious eyes of all outsiders, whether friendly or unfriendly; it was useless, even foolhardy, to peer into the shadowy darkness beyond.

It was clear that the drums, now rumbling louder — were they coming nearer? — were not making sweet-talk. And Linda needed no sixth sense to tell her that whatever affected the tribal have-nots would inevitably touch their benefactor: the Health Center.

And so it was with justifiable misgivings that she dressed hurriedly and went looking for Paul. Surely he would have an answer to this weird performance, though he had guessed wrong on at least one occasion. Paul had predicted that her first hundred days in the rain forests would be the hardest ones.

Those days had come and gone without untoward incident. True, they had been hard enough, but rewarding. The natives had been friendly, appreciative, eager to explore the modern ways of health as against magic potions and various primitive rites. And she herself had found love.

Locally, there had been little evidence of the unrest peculiar to a people groping their way out of darkness into light. But now, as the drums continued their spinechilling lament, Linda was convinced that the really hard days were at hand. What she had mistaken for apathy through the merciless heat of a seemingly interminable rainy season was about to erupt into violence.

The conviction grew as she passed through the corridors, the clinic, and peered into a classroom where a mere handful of student midwives awaited a tardy Peace Corps English teacher. She was greeted with the customary "Good morning, please, Missy," but each pair of dark eyes held a guarded look, and there wasn't a smile in sight.

There were no outpatients in the clinic — a strange thing at that hour. And although Sam and a few other native attendants were going about their duties in the wards as usual, they contrived to avoid questioning by remembering urgent business elsewhere when Linda drew near.

She found Paul and his senior associate in the research laboratory — also a strange thing at that hour, usually devoted to outpatients. They stood facing each other, conversing in low, guarded tones, as though the very walls had ears. The older doctor's face registered a mixture of grave concern and annoyance. Paul, freshly showered and shaven, immaculate in his hospital whites, looked none the less alert for his all-night sit-in with Research. He appeared to be highly indignant, even defiant. He was saying, his deep-South drawl accentuated by his anger:

"Wouldn't you just know they'd drum up a ruckus at a time like this, right when I'm on the verge of comin' up with something important? I no more than start making plans of my own when bedlam breaks loose, and I've got to start grubbin' all over again. Well, if this doesn't take the cake, I'll be a bobtail muley cow!"

"Oh, come now, Paul, save it," the older doctor counseled. "You know as well as I do that we'll have to forget Research for the time being. But this crisis will pass, so there's nothing to get excited about."

"Sure thing. It will pass — if only to make room for another one. No sense deluding ourselves."

"Exactly. Let's face it. We're going to have our hands full, what with the Peace

Corps being evacuated and our native help leaving in droves. Undoubtedly there will be bloodshed, and what will happen to our supply lines is anybody's guess." Dr. Armstrong, who had spent many years among underprivileged tribespeople, shook his head regretfully.

"Heck, don't these natives know who their friends are?" Paul exploded.

"How could they know? They've been exploited so long and by so many people, including their own."

"That's true," Paul agreed, and calmed down considerably. "But we've done nothing to hurt them. We're only beating our brains out trying to help. Maybe we should have our heads examined."

The older doctor smiled. "They know we're their friends. But this is their fight, and they want no outside interference. Human beings are funny that way. It's just our tough luck to be in the line of fire." He added in a conciliatory tone:

"Don't look so dejected, young fellow. It's too bad Research has to be our first casualty. I know how important it is to you get on with the work, now that you have an added incentive and are thinking in terms of marriage. But Miss Harlan will keep; she seems pretty durable." His eyes twinkled approvingly. "And love is like that: patient, understanding, long-suffering . . . "

"The heck it is," Paul blurted. "What would you know about love, at *your* age?" As a friendly joke, the remark fell flat, and Paul hastened to apologize. "Sorry, Doc. That was a putrid thing to say. I seem to be sort of wool-gathered this morning. But when a fellow finds love only to lose it — "

"Never mind the apologies. And you aren't losing it. As a matter of fact, you're running true to form. Too bad you young whippersnappers know so little about love." The old doctor chuckled. "It's the one common ailment that can turn a strong man — even a dedicated medic, begging your pardon, of course — into a jabbering idiot."

"Think so?" Paul retorted stiffly. "Then you won't be surprised to hear this: for two cents I'd give this miserable rain forest back to the witch doctors, throw in my microscope, become a guru, and set up practice back in the States.

Want to make something of it?"

"Horse feathers," the senior doctor commented, unperturbed. "All the evil spirits in Africa couldn't drag you away when you're needed."

13

LINDA, standing in the open doorway, increasingly uncomfortable in the role of eavesdropper but virtually rooted to the spot, turned to go. But her hope of slipping away unnoticed died aborning. Paul spied her, came forward and led her into the laboratory, closing the door behind them.

"Come join the guessing game, my dear," Dr. Armstrong invited. "But don't start asking what all the todo's about. Your guess is as good as ours, I suspect."

"Only the natives know," Paul said when they were seated, "and they're not talking. Cat's got everybody's tongue, including Sam's. All we know is, there's trouble afoot."

"Does it have anything to do with" — Linda hesitated, and her face flushed — "what happened last night? You know, Sam's doing away with that ghastly charm, and the tribeswoman running out on us? That was my fault, you know. Oh, Paul, if it's made trouble for you, I'll just die!"

Paul smiled and shook his head. That little episode, he assured her, was nothing more than a small straw in the wind of a gathering storm that could easily blow up in their faces. "Research is our first casualty, as it would be," he announced wearily.

"The current unpleasantness could be only a minor tribal hassle and blow over," Dr. Armstrong said, without conviction. "Although, according to rumors, there's a lot more than meets the eye. These things have a way of gaining impetus. We can only wait and see."

"One thing we do know," Paul said. "As the only public health unit this side of Beyond, we'll get the fallout, the victims. No guesswork about that."

There was no way of guessing what else lay ahead, considering the veil of secrecy that all but obscured the picture. For some time, Linda was told, there had been rumors of growing dissension among the various tribes. Quarrels were not unusual, but the wholesale bickering was taking on an ominous aspect. There were hush-hush stories of atrocities, human sacrifices, unconfirmed but credible.

Too, there were reports of a political upheaval, a military *coup d'état*, in the sprawling village that served as capital of the long-exploited province. It was rumored that all foreigners were to be evacuated, including the Peace Corps; whether by request or for reasons of safety, no one seemed to know. The Health Center, however, being a public service, surely would remain.

"The need for our facilities will be greater than ever in the uncertain days ahead," Dr. Armstrong predicted gravely.

There were any number of tangibles to support the rumors, such as; the funeral throbbing of drums, now assuming a martial tempo; the fact that native helpers and students were already leaving the Center, ostensibly 'to help my people,' but with fear written large in their faces. Most significant of all, perhaps, was the absence of Peace Corps volunteers from their self-imposed duties. So far today, not one had shown up, Paul pointed out.

"And we haven't seen hide nor hair

of our supply courier," he commented wryly. "All of which brings us back to the problem we came in here to discuss, Doc. Namely: what we'll use for help, space, medical supplies, when the shootin' starts. Come to think of it, I reckon Research isn't so important after all." He sounded so discouraged, so beaten, that Linda cried out with resolute brightness:

"Don't worry, Paul. We'll manage. There'll be three of us, at least, to carry on the work here; four, with Sam. He won't let us down, bless his heart!" She waited for Paul's approving smile, but his quickly averted face told her nothing.

"Only three of us, *with* Sam, my dear," Dr. Armstrong corrected. "Dr. Raymond and I have been talking the situation over. We feel you should leave with the Peace Corps group."

"No — *please!*" Linda gasped. "Is this an order? Am I being thrown out?"

"No. It's only a precaution," the old gentleman assured her. "We don't know the score yet, though we do have good reason to believe things will get a whole lot worse before they get better."

"But why should I go, when help is needed so badly?"

Paul returned to life, frowning. "Why?" he repeated, raising his voice. "For reasons of safety, birdbrain — *your* safety."

"Pooh," Linda scoffed. "The natives aren't mad at us; they're only mad at one another. You said so yourself."

"Never hear tell of the innocent bystander and what happened to him?" Paul, groaning aloud, turned his eyes heavenward in melodramatic appeal. "Good grief, I turn myself inside out trying to save her beautiful neck, and she wants to know *why!*"

"That's not funny," Linda announced hotly.

"It's not meant to be funny," Paul retorted, just as hotly. "You'll have to go, my darling."

"*Must* I, Dr. Armstrong?" In desperation, Linda appealed to the older man. He squirmed perceptibly, as if to say: "Look who's in the line of fire now!"

"After all," Linda continued, her voice stiffening, "it's *my* neck Paul — Dr. Raymond, I mean — is talking about.

If I choose to stick it out in the line of duty — ”

"The decision is indeed yours, my dear Miss Harlan," the senior doctor murmured. "Paul — Dr. Raymond, that is — should know that."

"Certainly I know it," Paul all but shouted. "But Linda — Miss Harlan, I mean — hasn't the faintest idea what she'd be letting herself in for if she remained here while the heat's on. From here on, there'll be nothing but drudgery, privation, danger . . . ”

"See what I mean, Dr. Armstrong?" Linda chimed in. "Paul — uh — Dr. Raymond thinks I can't take it. You heard what he called me just a minute ago. 'Birdbrain,' indeed! Oh, I got the message. He thinks I took up nursing for kicks!"

"No such thing, Doc," Paul bellowed. "It's only because I love her that I'm sending her away. Truth is, I'd sooner lose my right arm. But *you* tell her, Doc. She won't listen to me."

"Horse feathers," the old gentleman commented, as he had earlier. "Leave me out of this, will you? I'm telling nobody nothing," he added inelegantly.

"And while you're about it," Linda exclaimed incautiously, "you might inform that highhanded guru — Dr. Raymond, I mean — that I have no notion of freaking out at this point. I'm staying right here as long as I'm needed — never mind the hazards." She blurted, without thinking: "I hate to say this, Dr. Armstrong, but I'm in love with that" — she hesitated — "that character."

"Too bad." The old gentleman shook his head in mock commiseration, though his eyes twinkled. "I suspect Paul would be among the first to admit he's no prize package matrimonially speaking, now that Research is taking a beating. He isn't, you know — or do you?"

Instantly Linda was on the defensive. "You're joking, of course," she accused. "But how can you possibly find fault with the most wonderful man in the world?"

"Darling!" Paul beamed.

Dr. Armstrong rose to his feet and cleared his throat several times, but nobody paid any attention. The two erstwhile combatants were also on their feet, starryeyed and smiling, as though a cross word had never passed between them. In a minute they would be in each other's arms.

"Looks like it's a private war," Dr. Armstrong said to himself. "What the heck am I doing here?" With that, he stalked unnoticed out of the room, muttering something about the inconsistency of youth, and the unfairness of love and of war on innocent bystanders.

★ ★ ★

The days that followed were indeed rugged, and made all the more disconcerting by the hush-hush policy that prevailed. It was impossible to follow a normal routine; all one could count on was the unexpected, and gradually the unexpected became the accepted routine.

Each morning, after a few hours of intermittent rest, Linda would wake to the sound of double-talking drums, to face long hours of overlapping duties that left her numb from exhaustion. Sleep was a luxury to be indulged only in short takes, often fully dressed and always on call.

Yesterday's rumors became today's harsh realities as feuding tribesmen translated their grievances into spine-chilling shouts, body blows, knife thrusts and rifle fire. The small Health Center, getting the human fallout, was taxed to its utmost capacity. Straw pallets were placed in corridors and classrooms, where the smell of moldy grasses mingled with the more pungent stench of blood, sweat and antiseptics.

Now and then, further complicating the situation, groups of ailing refugees would drift in, having fled in terror from a new and unpredictable political regime. Such foods as rice, fish, fowl and fruits, obtainable locally, remained fairly plentiful. But there being no Peace Corps courier and little or no communication with the outside world, the shortage of medical supplies was increasingly acute.

Nevertheless, there were heartening aspects. Despite predictions to the contrary, many of the native helpers remained on duty, trying earnestly to compensate in willing service for lack of medical skill. Others came to offer their services or to bring rice and fruit from their own small stores. Unexpectedly, among the latter were Kali and Zalina, whose 'bedeviled' infant and missing charm had given Linda such a turn.

Beaming with motherly pride, the tribeswoman wore the sleeping baby strapped to her back, while her husband presented Linda with the biggest bag of rice she had ever seen in her life. There followed an avalanche of unintelligible words that left her speechless and brought Sam running to her rescue.

"They say baby is good, very good," the black boy translated obligingly. "Baby on earth to stay, so they start making ceremonial stool, cover it with lion skin."

"Good. What else are they saying?"

Sam hesitated, looking a trifle apologetic. "Kali, he say he name baby 'Paul' as favor to Young Doc."

"Why, that's fine, Sam," Linda exclaimed, touched.

Sam nodded soberly. "But never mind, Missy," he consoled. "Zalina already wearing more baby inside. She name him 'Missy' as favor for you. She say so herself."

Also on the brighter side, the clouds

became thinner, the rains less persistent, and there were other evidences that the rainy season was drawing to a close. Now and then an almost forgotten sun would peek out from behind a dawdling cloud, momentarily turning the soggy village streets into ersatz Turkish baths.

Later, as time passed, there were what Paul called 'previews or dress rehearsals' of the dry season ahead. Suddenly, as though some giant faucet had been turned, the rain would stop and, just as suddenly, there was not so much as a smear of a cloud in sight. Then the sun would come completely out of hiding — blinding, blistering — and in what seemed like no time at all, muddy lanes would become avenues of hard-baked clay.

On such occasions, barefoot pedestrians — mainly women and children and a few gaunt dogs — would emerge from their makeshift houses; glancing furtively around them while they performed outside chores, then scurrying back inside. Later, there would be fighting in the streets.

It was on such a bright, shining day that Sam announced, his eyes bugging:

"The devil, he will dance tonight. You will not see?" He looked from Linda to Paul in anxious appeal.

"Certainly we intend to watch." Paul laughed. Then, to Linda: "You haven't really lived till you've seen one of those weirdo performances. I'm sorry I have nothing more exciting to offer in the way of *divertissement*, But I'll arrange for box seats in the laboratory window. Be my guest, huh?"

"I'd love to," Linda said. "Sounds exciting. But *are* you sure we're allowed to watch?"

"Please don't, Missy," Sam implored. "There are no evil spirits, but — "

"Think we'll be struck dead?" Paul scoffed. "You may go now, Sam. Thank you for telling us about tonight's spectacular."

Sam, shaking his head unhappily, went on his way, while doctor and nurse returned to their various duties.

More than once through the busy afternoon, Linda found herself regretting her promise to join Paul in the dubious sport of devil-watching. Not because she was afraid, she told herself firmly. But it did not seem quite cricket for alien unbelievers to rush in where home-grown believers feared to tread. After all, devil-dances were strictly for the jungle gods — or so she had heard.

Each tribal village, she'd been told, had its official devil, whose identity was carefully guarded from the townspeople. Under orders from the paramount chief, he danced only in times of peril or imminent disaster, to propitiate angry gods; rarely, if ever, in times of joy. On such occasions every living creature remained inside, behind closed shutters.

Accompanying musicians were required to stand with their backs turned toward the dancing demon. Usually no arm-twisting was necessary to persuade foreigners to go along with the see-nothing idea. The savage rhythm alone, it was said, had such evil connotations that even the most dedicated Peeping Tom was reduced to goose pimples.

And so it was with some reluctance that Linda freshened her make-up and went into the laboratory at the appointed hour. The room, held free for major emergencies, was deserted, but a gallant attempt had been made to personalize it. All research equipment had been relegated to the background and shrouded with protective covers.

Furniture had been rearranged so that a table and wicker settee were grouped near a window. A vase of fragrant 'poor-man's orchids,' a bowl of fruit and a small bottle of palm wine added a festive note. The two desks — his and hers — were so innocent of clutter as to be almost unrecognizable. Only a telltale drawer oozing papers revealed the hurried masculine touch.

"Why, it's a party!" Linda exclaimed. "How in the world did he find time and strength to do it?" She wished now that she had changed from her working uniform into a dress worthy of the occasion.

She resisted a housewifely impulse to straighten out the mess of papers and close the desk drawer, fearful of displacing something vital to Research. Then, stepping over to a window, she looked out upon a scene that caused her to blink her eyes in disbelief. Sometime within the past half-hour or so, the village of Bugaboo had turned into a ghost town!

As far as she could see in the early twilight, shutters were closed on native huts, and there wasn't a living creature in sight: not so much as a hungry dog foraging for food, or even an enterprising rat.

Linda, shuddering, raised a hand to draw the window drapes against the gruesome scene. Hearing the door open, she lowered her hand quickly and turned to face Paul, hoping he had not seen the telltale gesture.

He came forward, smiling a little self-consciously; looking endearingly young in a white dinner jacket, his face flushed from over-close shaving and his absurd crew cut still wet from a quick shower.

"The late Dr. Raymond apologizes, Miss Harlan." Pulling a long face, Paul pretended to dodge a threatened blow. "Sorry, honey," he said, smiling again. "But there'll always be a time shortage, I reckon. There's never enough for a medic, you know. I'll probably show up late at our wedding."

"Well, you aren't late for this

performance. The show hasn't started, though the stage is all set. It looks pretty spooky outside. But in here" — Linda gestured — "it looks lovely: cozy, homelike, glamorous."

"Think so?" Paul made a deprecating gesture. "I wouldn't call it glamorous, exactly. But under the circumstances — "

Apparently sensing Linda's distaste for the scene outside — or was it in the interest of glamour? — he arranged the inadequate drapes so that most of the window was covered. Watching a devil-dance was an interesting experience for writers and students of tribal customs, he admitted, but a sorry excuse for an evening of relaxation. However, the important thing was, he told Linda, that they were together and alone for the first time since the uprising began.

"We have things to talk about, darling," he announced solemnly "We have considerable catching up to do in the romance department; promises to make, dreams to share, a wedding to plan. Time is flying and love is calling. What," he asked — with typical masculine unreason, Linda felt — "are we waiting for?"

243

Oh, well, I can be as obtuse as he can, Linda decided, taken aback by this abrupt approach and what appeared to be a planned assignation. Resolutely she ignored the prompting of her secret heart and searched her mind for an answer.

"We are waiting till your precious Research comes up with all the answers to everything," she said presently. "We are waiting for the day when there will be no more diseases to conquer, no wars, no sickness, no death; a day when all God's creatures will live forever, peacefully, happily."

"*That'll* be the day." Paul chortled.

"Yes. That will be the day, *our* day, if we live so long." Linda, close to tears, added quickly: "I'm sorry, Paul. I don't know what's come over me. I don't know why I'm saying such hateful things, but — " The words trailed off into a stifled sob.

Paul, looking baffled, tried to put an arm around Linda, but she moved out of his reach. "There, there, my sweet," he crooned. Then, in a normal tone:

"You're so right, darling. We've been operating like non-persons, robots; living other people's lives to the exclusion of our own. We're correcting that as of now. That's what I want to talk to you about. It's high time we gave our love a break by getting married as soon as we can." He grinned self-consciously. "If I don't make you happy, you can always throw me out. I'll cut my own throat."

"What a dreadful thing to say!" Linda gasped. "Marriage is a sacred thing, and love is for always."

"Right again, honey," Paul conceded seriously. "But love and marriage do not guarantee happiness. That is one of those will-o'-wisp things you have to catch by the forelock and enjoy as you go along. A lot of people don't know they've got it till it's gone. That mustn't happen to us, my beloved, my darling . . . " He stopped abruptly, then lashed out in self-condemnation:

"Heck, sweet-talk just isn't my media. Sorry, honey. I no more than open my mouth to make like a lover than I get tongue-tied, and nothing I say makes sense. What I'm trying to say is — " He spread his hands in a gesture of futility.

His self-criticism was justified, Linda

reflected. Many doctors, brilliant in their own field, were painfully inarticulate in affairs of the heart. Paul Raymond, she knew, was given to eloquent action rather than sentimental words. She would have to help him, she supposed.

"Why, you're doing fine, Paul, just fine — for a practicing physician." She frowned, realizing that she herself was not doing too well, but she continued sturdily: "What you're saying is that love is for always, while happiness is an elusive now-or-never affair. What I mean is," she stammered, "you have to take it as it comes — or else."

That didn't make sense either, she reflected unhappily, and took refuge in Paul's outstretched arms, burying her flushed face in the folds of his jacket . . .

14

THERE must have been a devil-dance on that moon-flooded evening which marked the beginning of stepped-up hostilities and the end of an over-long rainy season. And she, Linda, must have witnessed at least a part of the spectacle. At the time, it seemed like a passing nightmare superimposed upon a heavenly dream. Later, looking back, she could recall only the more salient details.

There was the moment when a fanfare of drums, growing in volume, signaled the approach of an advancing devil. Or was it the sound of silver bells, chiming in rhythm with two hearts that were operating as one — Paul's and hers? Even in retrospect, Linda could not be sure. It was impossible to separate one sound from the other, when the discord itself made music!

There was the moment when, safe in the shelter of Paul's arms, she peeked through the parted draperies and caught a glimpse of the performing demon. A faceless figure, made enormous by quantities of straw and feathers and all the more gruesome by psychedelic splotches of paint, he was snake-dancing along the winding lane that was the village's main street. With fiendish skill he was gyrating, posturing, collapsing, while accompanying musicians, walking backward and facing the other way, were giving out with a frenzied refrain.

At this point, Linda must have shuddered in fear, for the next instant Paul was kissing her eyes shut and walking her away from the window. He was saying:

"This is *our* night, my beloved. All the phony devils between here and Eternity can't spoil it. That goes for now — and always."

★ ★ ★

The succeeding days brought many changes to the rain forests, affecting the lives of many people. After a spurt of savage violence, a kind of precarious peace settled over the village. But all of Marimba, suffering the growing pains of a long overdue freedom, remained in a state of explosive unrest that boded no good for anyone.

The Peace Corps returned to the scene and resumed their humanitarian duties. But it was soon evident that the Health Center, always a calculated risk, would have to be abandoned. Unsettled conditions, outraged sponsors and lack of funds made full operation impossible. However, Dr. Armstrong, a benevolent Albert Schweitzer, avowed his intention of remaining on and doing whatever he could for ailing natives. Whenever feasible, critical cases would be flown to the nearest hospitals.

"It's what I want, my dear," the old gentleman told Linda when she deplored the loneliness and privation involved. "I've spent most of my life among the tribes. If I choose to spend the rest of it — "

Between native help and Peace Corps volunteers, he would manage, he assured Linda when she pointed out that even loyal Black Sam would not be around to do the heavy chores. Sam, torn between anticipation and regret, was getting ready to go to America for medical training — courtesy of the generous Christopher Osborne, the elder.

Paul, too, had his work cut out for him. Arrangements were being made for a large and handsomely equipped laboratory to be set up in the city of Monrovia, Liberia. And Paul Raymond, M.D., whose idea for on-the-spot research on tropical diseases was taking hold, would be top man.

As for their personal plans, Linda and Paul would be married at the family villa on Mamba Point, Monrovia, sometime during the forthcoming Christmas holidays. Then they would leave for a honeymoon in the States, combining business with pleasure. In Boston, Linda would renew old acquaintances and show off her bridegroom. And Paul, while showing off his bride, would attend medical confabs and speak on research at some of the teaching hospitals.

To Linda, it seemed a happy coincidence that one of Paul's scheduled talks was at Riverview, her alma mater. Nevertheless, she was taken aback when Paul suggested they write her old friend Gregory Arnold, reportedly in charge of research at Riverview, informing him of their plans.

"If only as a matter of courtesy," he explained. "What's wrong, sweet?" he asked when she shook her head vigorously. "Don't tell me you're still in love with that creep?"

"Most certainly not!"

"Okay, okay. I believe you. Then don't let's be persnickety. Since I'm supposed to sound off there and you'll be holding my hand, no sense walking in cold."

"That's true." Reluctantly, Linda agreed to write the letter.

★ ★ ★

It was mid-December, and the city of Monrovia, already dressed in holiday attire, was lovelier than ever. Or so Linda thought after her long and soul-testing sojourn in the remote rain forests. She had come on ahead, expecting to get some shopping done before Paul arrived for the wedding. He was still at the

Health Center, getting his things together and everything ship-shape for the closing of the main building.

Her first trip downtown was a mixture of enchantment and frustration. Flowers were blooming everywhere; the stores, large and small, were practically bulging at the sides with Christmas displays. In many cases, the gay Yuletide offerings oozed out onto the sidewalks, making walking difficult and shopping for such commonplace things as trousseaus impossible. And only a few more shopping days remained.

However, it was beautiful and heart-warming. Even the poorest houses wore seasonal emblems of peace and good will, fashioned of palm fronds, living flowers and brightly painted gourds; wore them proudly, happily, Linda observed as she taxied back to the villa, empty-handed but heartened.

The Harlan villa, too, in sharp contrast to the cold austerity of whitewashed hospital walls and strictly utilitarian furnishings, seemed more beautiful than Linda remembered. Outwardly, it was a little bit of heaven dropped out of the sky and equipped with all modern conveniences.

But there were times, inside, when it had all the qualities of a madhouse. The Christmas spirit was running rampant all over the place, while servants, on pre-Christmas behavior, were falling all over themselves and one another in their all-out efforts to please. In fact, Esther's customary aplomb was taking a kingsize beating, her smile growing a little thin at the edges.

There was still much to be done, Esther admitted wanly. There were boxes to pack for the worthy poor; other charity projects to supervise and execute, while doing her bit for her various altruistic group.

There was also the traditional Christmas Eve Open House at the villa, to be planned, accomplished, endured; not to mention the matter of getting young Suzy ready for school in the States.

"The dear child has changed completely since that unfortunate accident last year," Suzy's mother declared hopefully. "For some time she has wanted to do something in the way of social service.

Now she's decided to take up nursing as a career; feels she must finish high school and train in Boston, as you did."

Linda's jaw dropped, but she did not trust herself to speak.

"She admires you immensely, my dear," Esther said fondly. "She's getting to be a whole lot like you, Linda. Your father and I are quite thrilled."

"No, darling. She's getting like you: kind, thoughtful," Linda said, and hoped it was true. "But I'd dearly love to help you. Isn't there something I can do?" The question was no more than a friendly gesture. Everyone knew that the world's Esthers preferred to remain at the helping end of the line.

Esther shook her head. "No, thank you, my dear. I'll manage. With a trousseau to assemble and a wedding coming up, you have your hands full. If I really get stuck, your father is home till after the holidays. If I don't find something to occupy his time, he'll go out of his mind. I know he means well, but — "

Linda had to laugh. "I know what you mean, Esther. You'll go out of *your* mind if he doesn't get out from underfoot. Why don't you just haul off and tell him to get lost for a while?"

"Oh, I couldn't do that!" Esther gasped, shocked. "I'll find something. I'm not criticizing, mind you. But it is a little distracting, when you're trying to concentrate, to have a man around whistling the 'Wedding March' and singing 'Jingle Bells' off key. If only we'd made a tree this year instead of buying one that's already shedding — "

"And if I hadn't added a wedding to all your other problems — " Linda apologized. "I'm sorry, darling. Paul and I really should have made other arrangements."

Esther looked genuinely hurt. "Why, you couldn't possibly have done that to us, Linda, my dear. We're your family: Suzy, your father and I. And weddings are wonderful, no trouble at all."

It was the family consensus that weddings were wonderful, no trouble at all. But there was some difference of opinion as to what constituted a fitting wedding for a girl as lovely and beloved as Linda.

Esther wanted a garden wedding, with

flowering shrubs providing a natural altar and blossoming trees forming a fragrant archway against the blue sky. The guest list, she proposed, would include all the dear hearts and kindly people who were the Harlans' friends in their home away from home.

"That will include just about everybody in Monrovia, my love," Robert Harlan commented, smiling fondly at his wife. "We'll need the whole compound to accommodate the friends you've made. A garden isn't enough."

Esther smiled acknowledgement of the pretty compliment. "I'm not all that popular, love," she demurred. "Besides, we aren't likely to have too many guests at a Christmas week wedding. Most people have already made plans of their own. Yes," she said, with the uncompromising firmness of the outwardly meek, "it's all settled, darlings. Our lovely Garden of Eden is the perfect place for the wedding."

Suzy, who was present, giggled unashamedly. "What about the uninvited guests, Mom? You know — the mambas, tree cobras and things. But never mind answering." She snickered and tacked on with young audacity:

"All proper Gardens of Eden are allowed to have snakes, huh? They live there."

"Suzy!" Father warned. "Apologize to your mother."

Suzy did not apologize. Instead, she declared herself in favor of a for-real Christmas wedding, complete with Yuletide trimmings. The bridesmaids should wear costumes of red and green; the bride would be a living Christmas angel in illusion and white tulle.

"Well, it was good enough for Lynda Bird Johnson, wasn't it?" she retorted when Linda disapproved.

At this juncture Father, comparatively neutral up to now, rose to his feet and pointed an irate finger at the impertinent teen-ager. "Now look here, scatterbrain!" he raged. "If you're counting on me giving the bride away in a Santa Claus suit, you've got less sense than I've been giving you credit for."

Suzy shrugged. "I might have known you wouldn't co-operate. Old people are stuffy that way," she announced sulkily.

"In fact, if I were you, Sis," she told Linda, "I'd haul off and elope. There's nothing, but nothing, so romantic."

It remained for Chris Osborne to come up with the most startling suggestion. Chris, back on the scene and exasperatingly underfoot, took it upon himself to expound his views on the subject of weddings. Having recovered his power of locomotion, he had returned to Monrovia via India, where he had grown a beard and achieved a flowing hair-do while mastering the process of contemplation under the tutelage of one of the world's outstanding mystics.

In his gratuitous opinion, the wedding should take place in the quiet environment of the Osbornes' apartment at the Intercontinental, his father being away for the nonce. He himself would fly his personal guru in for the affair, Chris promised, thus assuring a ceremony that would be 'painless as well as spiritually rewarding' to everyone in attendance. It was the least he could do, he declared, in return for Linda's excellent nursing after the accident.

"Poppycock!" Father snorted when

Linda, shaking with laughter, told him about Chris' outlandish proposition. "Painless, indeed! Sounds to me like a jungle powwow, with everybody sitting around on the floor, cross-legged and unconscious. And there was a time when I was afraid you might be falling for that presumptuous young squirt."

He laughed, but Linda's face sobered. After all, there was a time when she had come perilously near to mistaking pity for a deeper emotion.

"Now, back to that wedding," Father was saying. "It's the most important event of your life, baby, and it really should be perfect in every way. And so, if I may make a suggestion — "

Linda pressed her hands to her ears. "*No — please*, Father! Whose wedding is this, anyhow? Don't Paul and I have anything to say about it? I'm sorry," she stammered, regretting the outburst.

When Paul arrived and she told him about the absurd controversy, he was amused but properly sympathetic. "We'll make our own plans, darling. All you need now is for your ex-sweet patootie to cable you, suggesting you change the whole operation, including the bridegroom."

Linda smiled sourly, but said nothing. No sense telling Paul that Gregory Arnold had done that very thing. It would only aggravate him as it had her.

Happily, there was no further controversy on the subject, and they made their own plans. They were married on the third day of Christmas in the little all-purpose chapel on United Nations Drive. Only the family and a few close friends were present when Paul Raymond, crusading doctor, and Linda Harlan, volunteer nurse, repeated their vows.

Everyone agreed that it was a perfect wedding: the bride beautiful, the clean-cut groom a mighty lucky fellow. Esther said as they came out of the chapel:

"I've never seen a prettier wedding or a lovelier bride. And I've seen them in all colors and in all parts of the world."

Suzy said: "He's a doll if ever there was one. I think his funny hair-do is sort of cute, and I've never seen such long lashes on a man."

Linda smiled to herself, remembering that Suzy had said precisely the same thing about Chris Osborne. Apparently it was the girl's fledgling idea of what constituted the perfect man. However, Suzy would learn — Linda hoped.

Christopher Osborne emerged from his soul-contemplation long enough for the customary amenities. Briefly he congratulated the bridegroom, wished the bride happiness, then resumed his other-world introspection. Black Sam, on a stopover en route to the States, was equally sparing of words, though the ones he spoke were eloquent with loyalty and affection.

"Missy and Young Doc," he intoned in careful English, "they are born for each other, and for a sick sick world where drums talk always of sorrow and need."

Father just beamed upon the happy couple, though the tears in back of his smile did not escape Linda. Aware that her own tears — happy tears — were showing, she tried with small success for a joke.

"Only womenfolk are supposed to cry at weddings, Dad," she teased.

Father tried, with even less success,

to be facetious. "Better cry now than later, baby." He became serious. "I hope you two research wizards have had the foresight to turn the microscope on yourselves. Have you examined your own minds, your hard-core opinions, your capacities for endurance, as well as your romantic hearts? Life isn't a perennial honeymoon — or do you know that?"

"We should know, sir," Paul said with confidence. "Already we've shared just about everything from witchcraft to war, not to mention a tropical rainy season."

"And you're still on speaking terms, eh? Good!"

"As for research, that hasn't been necessary," Paul continued. "I've known ever since I set eyes on your daughter that she's the one and only . . . "

"And we both know we love each other with all our hearts," Linda broke in, her smile meeting Paul's. "That's really all we want or need to know."

TO FIGHT THE WILD
Rod Ansell and Rachel Percy

Lost in uncharted Australian bush, Rod Ansell survived by hunting and trapping wild animals, improvising shelter and using all the bushman's skills he knew.

COROMANDEL
Pat Barr

India in the 1830s is a hot, uncomfortable place, where the East India Company still rules. Amelia and her new husband find themselves caught up in the animosities which seethe between the old order and the new.

THE SMALL PARTY
Lillian Beckwith

A frightening journey to safety begins for Ruth and her small party as their island is caught up in the dangers of armed insurrection.

THE WILDERNESS WALK
Sheila Bishop

Stifling unpleasant memories of a misbegotten romance in Cleave with Lord Francis Aubrey, Lavinia goes on holiday there with her sister. The two women are thrust into a romantic intrigue involving none other than Lord Francis.

THE RELUCTANT GUEST
Rosalind Brett

Ann Calvert went to spend a month on a South African farm with Theo Borland and his sister. They both proved to be different from her first idea of them, and there was Storr Peterson — the most disturbing man she had ever met.

ONE ENCHANTED SUMMER
Anne Tedlock Brooks

A tale of mystery and romance and a girl who found both during one enchanted summer.